DON'T WASTE MY TIME

TaKisha Trenean

For the lover in you...

CONTENTS

JULISSA

Mariah Carey's voice belted through my car radio as I sang along. The sun was bright and there wasn't a cloud in sight. It was a beautiful Saturday and I was heading over to my parents' house for brunch with them and my sisters. While waiting for the light to turn green, I used the opportunity to apply my mascara and lip gloss. For the first time in a long time I loved the person looking back at me in the mirror. I was working out, eating healthier and overall making both my physical and mental health a priority. The initial plan was to get my nails done but my mom had pushed and insisted that we all gathered together today. Based on both of my sisters' cars taking up the parking in the driveway, I knew that I was the last one to arrive.

"I hope no one gives me any flack about being late," I mumbled to myself before I made my way inside.

The tension in the air was... suffocating. It was obvious when I walked in that this wasn't a typical family get together and that I'd been the topic of discussion before I came strolling in. The house had been too quiet when I made my presence known. My family was loud, passionate, and lively; this house was huge, but it was never quiet.

"What the hell is going on?" I whispered to my sisters. When they didn't respond I looked to my older sister.

"Amara I know you know," I spoke through my teeth.

"And I think that you already know. You have to start taking care of yourself, Julissa"

1

"What the hell does that even mean? I do take care of myself." I narrowed my eyes and hissed.

"With the help of dad's money," Theresa, my younger sister chimed in.

"Oh, now you can speak Theresa?"

We fell quiet when my parents came to the table with their plates. Daddy carried his bill file under his arm. Great. The day had finally come. My dad had said the words I'd feared since getting my degree, well degrees. He was cutting me off. After receiving another credit card bill showing that I'd maxed out the card again daddy flipped. Luckily, I was spending his money and saving mine. Come on, I wasn't *that* spoiled. Honestly, my dad provided security, cushion. I could work or not work; take a risk on a business venture, or blow my budget for the month, but I could trust that all my bills would still get paid. My dad *always* took care of it. As a father of three girls he took care of all of us. I was the middle child and the most challenging if you let my parents tell it.

Flippantly I rolled my eyes. "Papí! Don't you think you are over-reacting just a bit?"

"Overreacting! Look at these bills Julissa!" My dad roared; his accent heavy. The loose papers flew across the table.

"Juan, honey, calm down before you raise your blood pressure." My mom patted his hand.

"Calm down? I have been through this with your daughter repeatedly. Why can't she be more like her sisters?" *And there it was.* Growing up I always felt like the black sheep, literally. I was the darkest one in my house and resembled my mom's youngest brother in both complexion and features. While they had straight hair, mine was curly and wild; untamable. My sisters wanted to take ballet and prance around the stage, and I wanted to do hip hop or karate. They spent their extra time in church while I snuck around with boys and my friends. They finished college and got married while I graduated and traveled. I didn't just go with what my parents told me to do. I questioned everything and always needed to know why.

"That's your real problem isn't it? Are we still on this? Your issue is that both of my sisters are married and I'm still out here fornicating without a ring on my finger isn't it?"

"Julissa, your mouth!" My mother gasped.

"Your mother and I didn't raise you to be a WHORE!" My dad slammed his fist on the table. Plates and forks shook and clanged.

My eyes shot up to my father's and I looked around the table waiting for one of these women to stand up for me. To defend me and my choices as a grown woman. To defend that being in tuned with my body and being sexual didn't make me a hoe. They all diverted their eyes to their plates, fucking traitors. My hands tighten around my fork so bad that it made my knuckles hurt. They were right about one thing. I needed to stop depending on my dad to take care of me and sponsoring lavish trips around the world.

"Despite what anyone of you think I am not a whore. I am sorry that didn't grow up to be who you groomed me to be and that I'm such a disappointment no matter what I do."

My voice shook but they wouldn't get a tear out of me. I was used to this even though I thought that we moved past it. My parents raised us in a strict Christian household. We were in church almost every day of the week from normal church service, to bible study, choir rehearsal, and youth group. We were raised to save ourselves for marriage and marriage was always the goal. Papí's girls weren't supposed to date unless the intentions were to get married. My sisters followed the path that was set for us and were both married. I'd lost my virginity at the age of sixteen. I was always the outcast of the family. Everything about me was edgier, the way I dressed, spoke, and wore may hair. Hell! My choice in men. I was the only daughter that dated outside of her race. My parents never said anything about it, but I knew it bothered them which was why they never met the men I entertained.

"Mom, dad, I wished that you didn't just love me because I am your daughter but also love the person that I am. You forget who comes over here and helps when either one of you are sick and these two selfish prudes are busy with their own families. I wish that you could see *me*." I nodded towards my sisters. I may have enjoyed spending my daddy's money, but I was dependable. I *always* came through when they needed me. My parents could rely on me.

"Julissa don't start the dramatics..." I threw my hands up.

"Of course. You don't have to take care of me anymore. I can manage on my own. My graphic design business is doing very well so I don't need your money or your approval. I'll just work even harder. Now if you all would excuse me; I lost my appetite and I have somewhere to be where I won't be judged and I am accepted for who I am."

As I grabbed my purse and headed towards the front door, I could hear my sisters protesting my departure, but it fell on deaf ears. They thought that they could just bash me and I was supposed to stay and take it, but my best friend taught me early on that I didn't have to take that shit and fuck people's opinions about me. As I headed to meet up with Lauryn and a few of our friends, I angrily swiped away at the tears that had fallen. Sometimes your closest family weren't always those related by blood.

I allowed the long drive and my favorite play list to calm my nerves. I was tired of having this conversation with my family. Tired of not being good enough or not meeting their expectations of me. My parents had done a lot for me, so I wasn't going to deny that. I'd never wanted for anything; anything I wanted or needed my dad provided. He owned several successful businesses and had made some lucrative investments. After my first year of college my dad gifted me with my condo against my mom's wishes. She wanted all of her girls to remain home until we got married. That was never an immediate goal of mine so I begged my dad to let me move out if I could prove that I was responsible, and I'd done that. Yeah, I had a slight problem with overly spending his money, but I was still a work in progress.

While my mom and sisters wanted to be wives and homemakers, I wanted to travel, drink, party, and have lots of sex and that's exactly what I'd done. I was nothing like my family; I was always different, and I was okay with that. While my sisters were home with a husband and kids, I was living my best life and creating memories. Truthfully, I was at a point in my life where I was maturing. My maturation process had a lot to do with my past relationship with a married man and my breakup with Brandon. Those series of events made me want to start taking my life seriously and working on myself. I really didn't want to have to depend on others, whether it was physically or emotionally. I'd started defining myself based on my relationships and that was not me. While Lauryn was adapting to married life, I worked on rediscovering myself. That included taking care of my health, doing things that made me happy, and changing my career trajectory. I spent a lot of time alone. It was important for me to live an authentic, holistic life, with a sprinkle of wild and crazy.

BIZZIE

Sprawled out on Jayna's couch, I made a few calls while I waited for her to bring BJ down. She'd moved back in with her parents after having our son. Everything changed after he made his entrance into the world and cried out for the first time. Being a father made me look at everything differently. There was some obvious bumps in the road but I was making it work. I was finally at a point where I was ready to go legit. I'd partnered up with Eric and his clubs, and I owned a couple of barber shops. In another month or so all my money would be clean, and I could hand over the business to Saint. He had more than proven himself loyal and worthy over the last few years; he deserved it. Honestly, I never thought this day would come. I'd plan to be in the streets until the streets took me, but my son changed everything. There was no way I wanted this type of life for him, so I had to lead by example and get my shit together.

"*What the hell is she doing*? Yo Jaynah! Jaynah!"

"What Bizzie? Why are you yelling like you don't have no damn home training?" She made her way downstairs with BJ on her hip and his bag on her back. I met her halfway, lifted BJ out of her arms and grabbed the bag. Jaynah had kept on some of the weight that she gained from the pregnancy, but it looked good on her. She was dressed in some little ass denim shorts, a white tank and no bra.

"Watch your mouth around my son, Jay. Is your dad here with you dressed like that?"

"No, they are out of town until Monday, so it is just me and BJ."

She gave a suggestive look and stuck her chest out. The hope was still evident in her eyes, but that ship had sailed. She'd slipped and showed her true self; I wasn't feeling the person that she revealed.

"Nah, that shit ain't happening Jay." I chuckled and shook my head. She poked her lip out in response.

"Why not?"

"Because you are manipulative as hell. Did you forget all of the hell you put me through? Besides that, I don't want to be with you in that way. We tried more than once, and we don't work and I..."

"And you what? For the love of God, I hope this isn't about that white bitch!" My eyes darkened and I rushed Jaynah, invading her personal space. Her eyes widened and she tried to move back but I grabbed her arm to keep her in place.

"I done told you about that shit. Let that be the last time you disrespect her, Jay. She ain't never done shit to you. Am I clear?" She snatched out of my grasp.

"Fine. Just have him back Sunday night."

"I'll drop him off to school on Monday and you can pick him up from there. You ready buddy?"

"Yes daddy!" He shook his head and smiled. I kissed my son on the top of his head and made my way out of the door.

When we walked into Eric and Lauren's mini mansion, I stopped and shook my head. The inside looked like a flower shop had exploded. Sis had transformed the first floor into the fucking garden of Eden. BJ kept trying to pluck the flowers, so I tugged his little hands.

"Yo B, you know the rules. Don't touch." With his head hung low, he poked his little lips out.

"Hey! There goes my little man."

Her scent made it over before she did. Julissa floated towards us, bent down and scooped up BJ. He smiled and giggled with glee as she planted kisses all over his fat cheeks and stuck her manicured nail in his left dimple. He melted in her embrace. BJ placed his hands on her cheeks and kissed her nose. They carried on as if I wasn't there. My heart swelled at their connection; they were smitten with each other and his mom hated it. I hated it at times.

She made my fucking chest hurt.

"JuJu!" he shouted.

Julissa smiled at him and they caught up like two old friends. I stood there looking stupid, feeling like a random bystander. I decided to enjoy the view. Julissa had lost a few pounds and toned up. She was still thick, just tighter in all the right places. Her hair was a different color and she wore it straight. Her fragrance was exotic and seducing, her signature scent. She was wearing a sundress with sandals and her nose was pierced, which was new. She was always put together well when out in public; she looked like a celebrity. Makeup flawless. Perfection personified.

"Brandon!" She stood with one hip popped out to help support BJ's heavy ass. She looked annoyed.

"This is not the place to be screaming my name, Ju. You know what that does to me. Now, if you play nice I'm willing to arrange something later on." I smirked and licked my lips.

"Shut up. Give me his bag, I'll take it up stairs." She ran her hands over BJ's wild hair before she placed him back on the floor. Julissa snatched his bag and jogged upstairs. My eyes followed her every move until she disappeared.

"Bitch stop drooling and go ahead and lock her wild ass down. You're embarrassing me man."

"Yo, fuck you, E." We both laughed and slapped hands before pulling each other into a brief hug. He squatted to greet BJ.

"What up little man?"

"Hi uncle! I want candy."

"Nah little man. You gotta eat first." Eric stood back up and straightened his shirt. He led me and BJ to the huge living area.

"You see this shit? Lauryn has gone crazy with the baby shower." Eric rubbed the back of his neck. He looked around the house like he was adding up the cost.

"That's your fault for spoiling her ass." We gave each other the same knowing glare.

Eric and Lauryn celebrated their third year of marriage last month and she was pregnant with their second child. Kinley and BJ where both two but BJ would be three in another month. With two girls in the house Eric didn't know the word no. Lauryn and Kin got whatever they wanted and this over the top baby shower was proof.

"Are you ready for another girl?"

"Hell, fuck no! Damn. Estrogen is starting to take over this damn house. Then Mrs. Taylor is here almost every other damn day. I appreciate the help but a nigga is backed up. Since you and Ju are here I might have to sneak my baby upstairs."

"Hey TMI nigga. That's my damn sister."

"She ain't yo real sister Biz."

"Don't tell my broski that. Hey Biz." Lauryn smiled and hugged me tight before lifting up BJ.

"Hey auntie baby. Look at you dressed like your daddy!"

"Man put his big ass down. What I told you about that?" Eric took BJ out of her arms and Lauryn rolled her eyes. She was glowing wearing an all-white dress and a damn flower crown. Motherhood suited her. She was great with both Kin and BJ. She loved my son like her own. The kid was lucky. Kinley shot by and ran circles around me while she giggled with pure joy. I scooped her up and peppered kisses on her cheeks, causing her to squeal and fall into another fit of laughter. Kinley hugged me then kicked her little legs until I placed her back on the ground. She sprinted towards the back door. BJ squirmed until Eric put him down. He took off outside behind his best friend. She didn't necessarily need a big brother and had BJ to look out for her. Lauryn lifted up on her toes and kissed Eric. The scowl on his face instantly vanished and I chuckled to myself. Married life had been good to my brother. He was now a family man, a great husband and father.

"Sooo....?" Lauryn poked at my chest and I frowned.

"So what?"

"Don't start." Eric warned but Lauryn ignored him, dismissing him with the wave of her hand. She rubbed his stomach to placate him.

"I know you've seen my best friend Brandon."

"Aight, that is it. Come on militant midget you got guests to entertain. You can bully Biz later. Biz, you know where the drinks are."

After thanking Eric, I made a beeline to the bar and poured me a glass of White Hennessey, then went to go check on my child. He was wild as hell, a ball of energy. They were outside playing on Kinley's swing set and calling it that was an understatement. My God daughter had a mini park built in the backyard equipped with swing sets and a bunch of shit to climb and jump on. There was even a damn teepee. Like I said, spoiled. As one of the many female guests caught my eye, I felt her brush past me. She hugged Lauryn from behind then lovingly rubbed her belly before making a beeline to the kids. Julissa was great with kids. They cheered when she approached them and begged to be pushed on the swings.

Since our post BJ's birth breakup, we hadn't said more than a few words to each other; mostly hi and bye. There was no one else to blame for that but me. I promised her that nothing would change with us but her worst fears came true after Jaynah had my son. She was adamant about not wanting him around other women and imposed a rule that I had to see him at her house, and I let her. I was spending more time at Jaynah's than my own place, which meant less time with Ju. After too many avoided fights, too many unanswered calls, canceled dates, and broken promises Julissa chucked up the deuces and moved on. There was no yelling or fighting just eyes filled with tears that didn't fall and me catching her sneaking out with a box of her things as I was walking in.

"What are you doing Julissa?"

"Not this. I'm done."

"Fuck Ju! I already told you that I can't do this dramatic shit with you. I have a lot on my plate. The last thing I need is grief from you."

"And that's it! That is the problem. You let Jaynah tell you what to do and give you hell, but I have to tiptoe around your feelings. I have to be your peace when there is a storm raging through me! I can't say that I miss you or how much it hurts when you cancel plans. When I do, you think it's because I don't understand your situation. You pushed me out of this relationship the day she took that baby home Brandon. I know you don't have time for this so don't say shit. I'm not asking for

you to fight for me anymore. You've already lost that battle..."

And just like that she was gone. She'd left her keys in the kitchen. Her scent, her essence lingered.

"OH shit!" The panic in Julissa's voice snapped me out of my thoughts. BJ had decided to jump mid swing and rolled in the grass. I was on them in no time. She was inspecting him as if she was a doctor. BJ was a tough kid but even my heart pounded out of my chest. I masked my fear because he would cry if I showed my true feelings.

"Chill, he's okay. You didn't break him."

"I'm so sorry. He's never done that before."

"Yeah that's some shit he picked up from his cousins on his mom's side. They got a bunch of boys. I've been teaching him to be a leader and not a follower." I squatted and look my son square in the eye. I could never deny my seed. He was every bit of me. The only thing he got from his mom was her hair. As soon as I broke eye contact, he was running back to play with the other kids. I stood up. Julissa turned to walk away but I grabbed her hand and tugged her back to me. A zap of electricity flowed between us and she snatched her hand back.

"How long are we going to do this Ju?"

"Do what?" Her cheeks flushed red and she avoided my eyes. She was flustered. Good. That meant that she still cared. There was still a chance for me to work my way back in. The way things ended with us hadn't sat well with me. I never set out to hurt her or not take our relationship seriously.

"Pretend that we don't know each other. Like there wasn't shit between us."

"Because its better this way. We tried and it was great while it lasted, but it didn't work." She shrugged and examined her nails.

"That's because you didn't give it time to work. You just walked out."

"Are you serious? Brandon, you didn't allow me the space to share how I was feeling and when I did you made me feel like I was stressing you out. I was killing myself holding that shit in while Jaynah slowly took you away from me."

"She could never take me away from you." Julissa tilted her head, narrowed her eyes, and crossed her arms.

"You're telling me that you haven't fucked her since we broke up?"

Damn, I wasn't expecting that. Julissa knew I wouldn't lie to her. She wasn't playing fair.

"Ju..." I closed my eyes and flinched. If I admitted to that it would be a bold face lie, but that shit was over. Julissa snatched her hand away. The hurt apparent in her brown eyes. She still cared. I felt like shit.

"I hate to hear that you were with her after me. I was hoping that I was wrong," she spoke in a soft tone.

"Yeah, I fell in that trap, but that's dead. Jaynah ain't you. You're my sweet and spicy Puerto Rican princess." My arms wrapped around her waist and I pulled her close. That elicited a smile out of her. I smiled back then enjoyed the view of her breast from being so close. She moaned and pushed out of my hold.

"Up here sir. You are trouble Brandon."

"And if I remember correctly, you like a little trouble. Let me take you out next week." She frowned and shook her head.

"Can't, I have plans. We shouldn't..."

"Fuck them plans, cancel them. We're going to work this out Ju and I don't share." I gripped her chin and pressed my lips into hers before walking away. She didn't say she was hanging with family or her girls, so I knew that meant she had a date. If she had any sense, she would cancel that shit before I did.

JULISSA

"**Y**ou don't think this dress is too much?" Lauryn's eyes met mine in the mirror.

"No, JuJu. First impressions are everything. Plus, your legs and boobs look great in that dress and those heels."

"This is not our first date."

"This is your first date that doesn't require casual attire. He needs to know what you're working with!"

"Girl Ethan already knows what I'm working with." I smiled and licked out my tongue.

"You dirty, dirty girl. You been holding out on me."

Lauryn and I went shopping earlier and picked out an all-black bodycon dress that hugged all of my curves and highlighted my ample cleavage. My hair was back in its natural curly state and I got a natural beat done at the makeup counter in the mall. My emotions were all over the place. Seeing Brandon at the baby shower threw me off. I'd thought I'd prepared myself to see him again, but I was not ready to be face-to-face with him and all his sexiness; I wasn't ready. I was never attracted to bigger guys until I met this man, but Brandon was big and fit; complete eye candy worthy. He smelled good and looked good enough to eat from his contagious smile, to the tattoos that ran up his arms and neck.

After our breakup I continued to make horrible decisions regarding my choice in men. For a long time I thought that my worth was defined by a man's love or attraction. There was my grad school professor who had a penchant for fucking his students, catch the plural, the stripper, which was enjoyable until his biggest fan slashed my tires and stalked me, and last, there was Lauryn's old friend Trey who I doubled back on, more than once. Don't judge me. Anyway, I was trying to avoid adding anyone new to my body count, not that I cared what anyone else thought. I just didn't want to waste this bomb ass cookie on another dude who was undeserving of all that I had to offer, both inside and outside of the bedroom. That was until Ethan who grooved his way into my life with his perfectly constructed words and melodic voice. Ethan was the first guy in a long time that made me feel safe and secure. He was a middle school English teacher and a poet. I met him at one of Eric's lounges where he performed on open mic night. The man had a way of putting together words that had women clinching their thighs tight and squirming in their seat. I liked him, a lot. Ethan was smart, kind, respectful, had a normal job, and no baby mama drama; he was *safe*. We'd been dating for a few months now and I couldn't find anything wrong with him.

"This dress does make my titties look good, don't it?" I squealed and smiled in Lauryn's direction.

"Did I stutter? Anyway, share your location with me just in case we have to run up on him."

By *we*, Lauryn meant her and Eric. A few months ago, I had the date from hell. I'd went out with a guy who I'd met at the gym and he showed his entire ass. First, he was too flashy. He wore an obnoxious amount of gold jewelry. Second, he wore a Versace shirt that took me back to the 1990's, it was just plain ugly and drew even more unwanted looks. This dude got drunk to the point that he became irate and disorderly. I tried to get him to settle down, but that only seemed to escalate him. He had a grip on my arm and wouldn't allow me to leave the restaurant. By his fourth drink I'd already texted Lauryn the SOS signal, I just didn't expect to see Eric barging over to our section. As he approached us he looked annoyed. That was until he looked down and saw dude's hand on me then his eyes darkened and anger took over. Eric and I had gotten extremely close over the years and he took on the role as protective big brother. Before dude knew what was happening Eric rocked him dead in the jaw. Blood spewed from his mouth and he flipped over the table causing a scene. Ever since then I couldn't dare go out with anyone without Eric and Lauryn vetting them first. They'd both met Ethan and although neither had warmed up to him they didn't get any creepy vibes from him.

"It's beyond me why you still don't like Ethan."

"It's not that I don't like him. He's a nice guy, I just don't like him for you. What you need to do is give Bizzie another chance because what I'm not going to do is let you sit here and tell me you don't still have feelings for him."

"First of all, you have a soft spot for that man. And second, what *I'm* not going to do is talk about that man right before my date. Brandon had me and when our relationship was tested, he failed, miserably. Did you know he went right back to fucking her?" I shoved the essentials in my small purse and ignored that know-it-all smirk that I knew Lauryn was wearing. She thought she knew *everything;* well she did know me. Lauryn sighed and stood up. She hooked her purse on her shoulder.

"Okay I won't push, today. Come and walk your pregnant friend downstairs. The baby is hungry."

"Does the baby want auntie to make her a sandwich?" I rubbed her perfectly round belly as I spoke to it. She kissed her teeth and brushed my hands off of her.

"Hell no! This baby wants a three-course meal from the restaurant that her daddy is going to leave work early to take me to."

"And to think, people say that I am spoiled." I hugged Lauryn and gave her an air kiss to not mess up my glossy lips.

"Favor ain't fair." She sang and stuck out her tongue.

"Call me when you get to Eric."

"Yep. Bye Ju."

It was perfect timing because as soon as one elevator closed the other opened and Ethan stepped out. I'd given him my personal code so that he could get in with no hassle. He looked surprised to see me standing in the hallway. He smiled and swaggered towards me. He was wearing blue pants, a rust colored jacket over a Jimi

15

Hendrix t-shirt, and rust colored Vans. Ethan's style was eclectic and it fit his personality perfectly.

"Hey beautiful."

"Hi! Um, Lauryn just left. You can come in. I need to grab my things and lock up." I paused before turning around. "Are those for me? Ethan was holding a bouquet of red roses. They were definitely *not* my favorite, but I kept the smile plastered on my face as he handed them to me.

"Yes, they are."

"Thank you."

I made a quick task of placing the flowers in a watered vase then grabbed my purse and keys. Before I reached the door Ethan pulled me in to his arms and kissed me. It was slow, deliberate, and sensual; he was an amazing kisser. My arms snaked around his neck to hold him in place. We made out like two horny teenagers until my phone rang. I chose to ignore it but it was enough of an interruption to pull us apart. Ethan opened the door and tugged my hand.

"Come on, let's go."

"Are you enjoying your food?"

"Mmm hmm. This is the best Greek food I have had. Well besides when I went to Greece. There is no comparison."

"You've been to Greece?" Ethan looked up at me with interest.

"Yes, I toured Europe one summer. Greece by far was my favorite country."

"Greece is alright but I'm more into touring the African continent."

"Oh I've been there too." I gazed at him knowingly. He was not about to play me like I was some basic chick.

"Oh yeah? Where you been, South Africa?"

"Actually yes, but also Nigeria and Ghana."

"See, I knew there was something I liked about you."

"Yeah, there's more to me than what you see on the surface."

The restaurant was an entire vibe; more than what I was expecting. It was a new Greek spot that had just opened up. It wasn't really Ethan's thing, but he heard me talk about it enough to know that having dinner here would please me. The décor was minimal and colored in natural woods, greens, and blues. The conversation was easy and intriguing. Ethan read a lot and could talk about anything. He appealed to my inner nerd and we were having a great time. It was so great that I was oblivious to what was about to happen.

"I see you like testing me, Ju. I thought I told you to cancel the date."

My eyes bulged and I choked on my chicken. Ethan made a move to assist me but stopped.

"Hell nah, playboy. She'll be alright; she ain't dying. Julissa what the hell are you doing?"

Brandon grilled me. I was at a loss for words and honestly still trying to catch my breath. I'm pretty sure I looked like a damn deer in head lights. Ethan sat back down and addressed Brandon, asking who he was. The only thing that was running through my mind was prayers. Prayers that Brandon didn't lose his shit in front of all of these people. Brandon was mild mannered, but he wasn't Eric's muscle for nothing and his temper could flare when the right buttons were pushed. Lord help us.

BIZZIE

"Julissa is my girl." I snarled. I felt like I was shooting out flames. I was heated. I stood outside the window and watched her laugh and smile with this old poet ass lame. We never talked like that and it had me feeling some type of way. I ignored the daggers she was shooting at me with her eyes.

"Yo, my bad. I had no idea. Julissa, what is going on?" The dude held his hands up in surrender.

"Of course you didn't, but now that you know why the fuck are you still here?" The dude tilted his head and bristled. If he knew what was good for him he would think twice about jumping back at me.

"Brandon! Ethan I am *not* his girl. He is certifiable. You are not wrapped to tight Brandon."

"Okay and? You just discovering this shit?"

I was ready to cause a scene in the bitch and I would if one of them didn't get their ass up. Normally, I wouldn't sweat a female this hard, but this was Julissa and I wasn't going another day without her being officially mine. The waitress was already speaking to the hostess and pointing in our direction. Julissa was playing hard ball and trying to convince her date to stay. I leaned over until I was at her ear.

"Yo if you don't get your ass up now, I am going to pistol whip his bitch ass all over this restaurant. Matter of fact, I don't even need that. My fist will do. He don't look like he can afford to

18

have his jaw wired shut." When I flashed my piece Julissa huffed, grabbed her purse and stormed out of the restaurant with me close behind. When we were both outside and on the sidewalk she hauled off and slapped me.

"Fuck you Brandon! Are you fucking crazy? You had no right!" Her anger did nothing but turn me on. A grin formed across my face as I held my jaw.

"I should slap that smug ass look off your face." I took two steps until we were toe-to-toe.

"I want you to try. I already let you get one off, that won't happen again." I had to admit that she looked good, but she got all dressed up for another man. It would be her last time.

"Why are you here? How did you even... Lauryn. How did you get her to tell you where I was?" Julissa stomped her foot like she was having a tantrum.

"It really wasn't that damn hard, but that ain't the point. The point is I told you to cancel your plans."

"Just because you tell me to do something doesn't mean that I'm going to do it! Nobody tells me what to do! I only left because I didn't want to drag Ethan into this bullshit. If you think that this is the way to win me back, you are fucking delusional." I licked my lips and took in her appearance again. The sexual tension between us could be cut with a knife.

"Your body's reaction tells me otherwise Ju."

With that she spun around and headed to her car. Before she pulled off she gave me the middle finger. My hand rested on the side of my face that still stung at little from her slap. I hopped in my Challenger and made my way downtown.

JULISSA

My door slammed behind me and I screamed in frustration. I'd done a pretty good job at avoiding Brandon until Lauryn's baby shower. Now I couldn't stop thinking about him and he wasn't making it any easier. Truth be told, I left a piece of me at Bizzie's apartment when I walked out almost three years ago. I'd hoped that he would come after me, fight for me, but he didn't. He simply moved on and broke my heart, but I could not deny that I still loved him. It was partially why I loved his kid so much. I couldn't help but love someone that was an extension of him, but little BJ was easy to love anyway.

I kicked off my Prada heels and trudged to my kitchen. A shot of tequila was in order. After taking two shots I wiped my mouth with the back of my hand. My throat burned but I welcomed that warmth that filled my chest. I instructed Google to play something I like and Alicia Keys *If I Was Your Woman* flowed from the speakers. Her sultry voice soothed my spirit as I danced around my condo.

If I was your woman
And you were my man
You'd have no other woman
You'd be weak as a lamb

This woman's music spoke to my soul and put me in a zone. I was ready to love hard and have that equally reciprocated. There were too many instances where I had to fight for reciprocity. I did too much, poured too much of myself into men who shitted all

20

over me. All they ever seemed to do was drain me. Brandon did it emotionally. At some point in our relationship he decided that he would give me whatever he had left over after he was done with BJ and Jaynah. He'd checked out on me. I was built to love; I had so much to give.

Releasing a shaky sigh, I removed my bra without taking off my shirt and tossed it in my room. The knock on my door caused me to frown and do an about face. My brows furrowed even more after looking through the peephole. My heart slammed into my chest and I gasped for air. I ran my hand through my hair to tame my wild curls. I cleared my throat, stood up straight and slowly pulled the door open. Brandon stood on the other side looking just big and sexy. Brandon was a big dude; he took up space wherever he went. He was muscular and tall and gruff. He was dressed in all black with a simple gold chain and watch. He smelled like sin and bad decisions. Brandon smiled and made his way in as I involuntarily stepped back to give him room to enter. I closed the door and gulped.

"What are you doing here?" I blinked and he had me pinned against the front door. His hands roamed all over my body as our lips collided. His tongue darted into my mouth when I gasped for air. He tasted like weed and cognac. *Damn, I'd missed the combination.* My body was on fire and his huge hands left goosebumps in its path. We ripped at each other's clothes until we were both bare and exposed. Brandon lifted me around his waist and headed towards the kitchen. My ass smacked against the kitchen counter and I tried to catch my breath while he slipped on a condom. He flattened his tongue and licked up my neck while he entered me. He filled me like no man ever could; the feeling was unmatched. We both released a collective sigh and neither one of us moved.

"I missed you so fuckin much." He growled in my ear before he pulled out and slowly eased back in, making me feel every inch of him. I whimpered and let my hair fall on his shoulder. This slow and soft shit, I didn't want. Brandon was trying to say more with his body than he could with his mouth. I just wanted him to fuck me senseless. I wanted to feel but not emotionally, just physically.

"Bizzie." I whined. He worked his pelvis in a circle, stirring up my nectar.

"Oh I'm Bizzie now." He grunted before capturing my mouth. I was totally high off of this man and irreparably in love with him. Our bodies moved in sync as I met him thrust for thrust. When I rolled my hips, arched my back and pushed back into him he groaned in my ear. Sounds of our love making drowned out the music as we reached our peak together.

"Fuck Ju."

"Oh shit Biz!"

My psyche snapped and I cried out in euphoric pleasure as my body convulsed and I milked his dick until he filled the condom. Brandon held me tight and I could feel both of our hearts pounding. He pulled the stool from under the counter and plopped down. He kissed my thighs with his full lips.

"Dammit baby." A lazy smirk graced my face and I planted my hands behind me to brace myself on the counter. Our session had zapped all of my energy and I was struggling to stay upright. I felt his body press against me again and he lifted me off the counter.

"Come on light weight, let's wash up."

I sat on the side of the tub expecting Brandon to turn on the shower. My eyebrow arched when he started to run water in the tub. He busied himself with adding my bath bomb and a little bubble bath. It warmed my heart to know that he still remembered where I kept everything. When the tub was full, I tested the water with my feet then slowly slid into the water. A moan escaped my lips. I closed my eyes and enjoyed the heat from the water and the smell of lavender and honey.

"Scoot that ass up."

"Huh what? What are you doing?" Brandon slid in behind me and I rested my head on his broad chest. I used to always ask him to take baths with me and he would always refuse and reply with, "That's some pussy shit."

"Shut up and enjoy it. I need to soak anyway. My body is sore from working out."

"Why are you so mean? Rude ass." I slapped his arm and laughed. Brandon's biceps were huge and I felt invincible and protected whenever he wrapped his arms around me. He simply grunted and kissed the side of my face. There were two different sides to this man; the Gemini in him. There's Brandon who was affectionate, passionate, loving and sometimes funny. Then you had Bizzie who was rough around the edges, intimidating, rude as hell, but fiercely protective. I was getting a piece of Bizzie right now. He needed the silence; he was masking something.

Freshly bathed and moisturized we laid in the middle of my bed. We were snacking on a bowl of grapes since my date didn't make it to dinner. I was going to need an early breakfast in the morning. I pretended to feed him a grape then snatched it away and ate it myself.

"Why you always gotta play? Your childish ass."

"Oh, so I'm childish now?"

"Look at you! Lion King t-shirt and Wonder Woman socks?"

"Damn, tell me how you really feel. Sorry that you don't think my attire for bed is sexy." I lifted the empty bowl and took it to the kitchen. When I came back into the bedroom Brandon motioned for me with his head.

"Come here."

The deep rumble of his voice made my kitty throb and salivate. I did my best sexy walk over to the bed before I climbed up and straddled him. His calloused hands slipped under my shirt and he moved his thumbs around my stomach. I held on to his huge biceps and waited; he was ready to talk.

"I missed you Ju." I opened my mouth to respond and he shook his head to stop me.

"When BJ was born something in me changed. My heart began to beat a little bit stronger and for the first time I had my own family; my blood. When I first held him and he looked up at me I vowed to provide him with the life I never had, to protect him from this world for as long as I could. I wanted to teach him what family should look like and I still feel that way but I handled that shit wrong back then. I fucked up. I gave Jaynah too much power in how I moved with you. I didn't realize how much you were a part of my family until you were gone. Letting you walk out of that door was the biggest mistake I have ever made. And even with all the shit I put you through after promising to protect you from that drama you still had room to love my son. BJ gets something from you that he doesn't get from me and Jay. It's the same with him, Eric, and Lauryn. Thank you for that. Thank you for pouring into him; for being a part of his village. That's the kind of woman that I want in my life.

"My son healed me from unresolved childhood shit but then you left and a piece of me was missing again. I missed your strength, the way you love, these childish t-shirts and socks. I actually love your pj's."

He tugged at the hem of my shirt. "Your ambition, and excitement for life. I need that type of energy around me. I can't continue to go every day without it. Shit, I say all this to say I don't want you to wake up tomorrow questioning shit. You are mine and nothing or no one will ever come in between that again. I'm sorry."

For once I was the one without words. My hand rested on my chest while I just stared into his eyes. The emotion behind them rendered me speechless. I *was* ready to be loved and I wanted it with him. It was hard to grasp that we were finally here. Even with what I was feeling, I still wasn't a hundred percent sure that he wouldn't hurt me again, but I couldn't deny that this moment and what we were both feeling was real.

"I love you Ju."

A sob escaped my mouth and I cried like a baby. Brandon embraced me and massaged my scalp until I calmed down. I sat up and held his face between my hands.

"I love you so much."

"Julissa?"

"Yes?"

"I'm going to fuck the shit out of you now." I yelped when he ripped my panties off and eased me down onto his erection. A mischievous grin fell upon my face and I braced myself for the ride of my life. Who was I to deny him?

The next morning, we woke up and worked out. I quickly reminded myself to say no the next time Brandon suggest we work out together. He was a beast and pushed me to go just as hard as he did. That only led to us arguing and me stomping off, but we made up in the shower. Now I was sore and my coochie felt swollen. I limped into the kitchen and Brandon chuckled.

"What's so damn funny?"

"You. You want me to cook breakfast so you can rest?"

I kissed my teeth and twisted up my lips. When I finally took in his appearance he was wearing sweatpants, showing all his glory and blessings.

"Where did you get those from? Did you already have those in your car or did you pack a bag?"

Brandon shrugged his shoulders and ran his hand down his stomach. *He'd packed a bag.*

"You are crazy." I scoffed and shook my head.

"Only when it comes to you. Matter of fact, make sure you delete and block that nigga from your phone."

"Brandon!" Brandon gave me that intimidating, no nonsense look he was known for. When I tripped over my own foot on my way to the refrigerator, he made his way into the kitchen.

"Man have a seat and let me handle this." He leaned down and kissed me on my lips and tugged my bottom lip between his teeth before he pulled away. I loved that I got the privilege of seeing this side of him. I just prayed that it lasted. Not one to argue with a man who was willing to cook I smiled and hopped up on the stool and watched him work.

• •

It was a Friday night and I was home finishing up a project that I'd first procrastinated on then struggled with some of the coding for my client's website. He was an artist and wanted the design of his website to represent his artistry and personality. The intricacies of the site was complicated but I had no doubt that I could do it. I had to come through at this point. I'd promised a finished product by Monday. Brandon and I was supposed to be spending tonight at the Improv with Lauryn and Eric so I was bummed about having to cancel. This would have been Brandon and my first date since we decided to give it another shot. Although he didn't want to, I insisted that he go without me; he needed time for himself.

I'd been at it for hours. Sitting in my designated office area, I was dressed in a t-shirt and sweats. My hair was pulled back in a loose ponytail. Once I felt that I had all the kinks figured out I loaded up my clients website and held by breath. When the site loaded with a slideshow of some of his most popular artwork I released a sigh of relief and scooted back from my desk.

"Thank God!" I exclaimed. I stuck my hand into the Wonder Woman bowl next to me and stuffed my mouth with popcorn and Reese's Pieces. As I did a quick spin in my office chair, keys jingled at my door. When the door eased opened I was facing it, my chest heaving from the rush. Brandon stood there looking sinfully handsome wearing dark slacks, a button up, and what looked like an expensive pair of shoes. He wore a gold Cuban link around his neck and a matching watch. We looked like night and day.

"Hey! How was the show?" I pushed off from the desk and the chair rolled towards Brandon but stopped a few feet short. He shook his head and smirked in my direction.

"It was funny as shit. You would have loved it. We missed you."

"I know, but at least I got my work done. Next time I won't wait to the last minute. Business has increased so I need to be more deliberate about planning my days. I might even need to hire another assistant or an intern. Do you think I need to rent a workspace?"

Brandon didn't respond immediately, but instead pulled me up from the chair and wrapped his strong arms around me. We both leaned into a sweet kiss. His hands moved down my body and grazed my thigh.

"Yeah. You have outgrown the home office and with your own space you can actually have your clients come to you."

"I can do that here."

"No you can't." There he was giving me his signature stoic expression. "I can help you look for some places. Any plans tomorrow?"

"No but..."

"But what Ju?"

"I really want to do this on my on, you know. No handouts. As much as I appreciate the offer. I can't. I've been letting my dad support me like a crutch for too long and I don't want to do that with you. I don't want to depend on you in that way." Brandon stepped back and headed towards my kitchen.

"Julissa, I'm your man and I want to take care of you. Besides, I have the means to do it. Let's at least commit to looking up places tomorrow; no pressure to make any decisions. I'll shoot a message to my realtor."

Based on the way Brandon turned his back to me as if the conversation was over, I knew that I was fighting a losing battle. His mind was made up and there was no changing it. I appreciated his offer, but I had to find a way to do this on my own. My family would always see me as a disappointment if I went from taking money from my father to allowing Brandon to take care of me. I opened the refrigerator and grabbed a bottle of pomegranate juice.

"Fine, okay. Sure."

"Trust me Ju. I got you."

BIZZIE

"Yo lil man. Come here so I can put your shoes on. Your mom should be here soon.

"No! I want to stay." BJ stomped his foot and his eyes filled with tears. I hated when he got like this. There were somedays where he had his bag waiting at the damn door like he had a horrible time, but most days, like today he was extra attached to me. He was clingy today and followed me around like he was my shadow. That was until I told him to get ready.

I walked over to him and squatted to his eye level. He looked everywhere but at me and kept trying to run back to his toys.

"Hey, my man, focus. Look at daddy. It's time to go back home with your mom. Daddy will come and get you in a few days to hang out. I promise. Okay?"

"Okay."

"Aww you can do better than that. Say it like you mean it. Say it with your chest!"

"OKAY!" BJ yelled to the top of his lungs and just like that, his smile was back on his face.

"That's what I am talking about. Now let's get these shoes on."

BJ ran and climbed up on the chair. By the time I tied his last shoe the doorbell chimed. That should be ya moms. I pulled the door open and Jaynah stood there typing on her phone. When she looked up her face was filled with disdain.

"Where's my baby?"

"He's inside. Come in for a minute, I need to talk to you."

"Okaaaay." Her eyebrow raised in suspicion. I held the door open and motioned for her to join our son in the living room.

"Mommy!"

"Hey big boy. Mommy missed you!" He ran to his mom like he wasn't just crying about wanting to stay with me. My son was far from being a mama's boy but he loved his mother more than anything. She kissed the top of his head then stood.

"What do we need to talk about?" Her eyes held a flicker of optimism that I was probably about to kill.

"I ain't one to beat around the bush so I will spit it out. Julissa and I are back together. We're working things out."

"Seriously? What is it about that white..." Her words faded when our eyes met. Disrespecting her like that wasn't going to be tolerated.

"What is it about her that makes you say fuck me? Why can't you love me Bizzie? I gave birth to your son!"

"Jay this ain't about you. I can't help how I feel about her. She brings something in my life that I never knew I needed. We work and it is effortless, not forced. It's time for you to move on and find your own happiness, Jay. As much as I want that for you, it ain't me."

She crossed her arms and refused to speak, so I continued.

"Julissa will respect you and you will respect her. Don't give me shit about our son being around her. You know he's safe with her. You won't talk shit about her in front of anyone, especially not BJ. He loves her, Jay. Don't take that away from him. Understand?"

She stood and picked up both BJ and his backpack. I noticed the slight nod of her head. Her nose was red and her lips trembled.

"Yeah I hear you, but you better be sure about her and this."

With that I escorted Jaynah and my seed to the door. I placed a kiss on his forehead.

"You take care of you mom. Oh, I promised that I would get him one day this week."

"That's fine, just text me." Not waiting for a response, she turned and headed for her car. It was our routine that I helped her get BJ in the car but I figured she wanted me out of her face so I let her be. Dispelling a rush of air, I wiped my hands down my face. I needed to unwind so I placed a quick call to Eric to see if he was at the lounge before making my way over.

"Y'all finally doing this shit, huh?"

"The Puerto Rican princess finally gave in and gave ya boy another chance." I couldn't help the triumphant grin that formed on my face. When Julissa and I first broke up it was bad. She didn't even want to be in the same room with me for a while. The shit made me sick. Truthfully, I fucked up royally and wounded her with the stunts that I was pulling, I couldn't be mad at her initial reaction. I still don't know how I was able to make it happen because before the baby shower we were only on a hi and bye basis. There was no point in dwelling in the past. We were back on track and she was my present and my future.

"Do you think Ju is the one?"

I nodded with certainty. "Yeah, I think so. We're so different, but we still fit perfectly."

"She's good for you. Fire and Ice." I sipped my drink and waited. I knew my friend and there was more on his mind.

"What man?"

"You really think Jaynah is cool with this? She hates Julissa and hates that she ain't black even more."

"Her problem with Ju is beyond me. I told her what it was and she said that she would chill so." I shrugged my shoulders. Eric shook his head and leaned forwards in his seat.

"I don't know Biz. Baby momma gave in too easily for me. You better keep an eye on her."

"Nah she will be on her best behavior. She will be looking for any reason to pop off but Ju won't give it to her."

"You think Ju could take her?"

"Man what?" Eric pointed the wing he was feasting on in my direction and smiled at me deviously.

"If shit went left do you think Ju could handle her? I think she could. Jay would automatically underestimate her and you better hope that Lauryn ain't around when it happens."

"Lauryn? Fighting? Nah, I don't see that."

"Yeah you forgot, I've seen it firsthand and she don't play about her best friend."

Me and *my* best friend were hanging out at a spot we owned together along with Kevin, Blue Lounge. It was now the hottest spot in town and was frequented by all types of celebrities. To top it off the food was good as hell. The lounge was opened daily and the vibe was low key except for the weekend. Things picked up Friday, Saturday, and Sunday nights and we hosted a daytime party on Saturday and Sunday. Business was good and life was better. At this point, I couldn't ask for anything more.

"Yeah, she did jump on Tash, didn't she? And she took out that other chick. What was her name again?"

"We ain't talking about that crazy shit. Lauryn still isn't fully over that. She's more guarded with who she makes friends with, which I ain't complaining about, and she is very protective when it comes to McKinley."

"I don't blame her. Sis went through a lot of crazy shit. Most of it because of you." I nodded my head in Eric's direction and he did the same.

"Yeah, alright, but all that shit is in the past. We came a long way."

"Indeed."

We spent the rest of the night enjoying our drinks and vibing to the music until wifey called with a late-night craving and Eric had to dip. I took my time driving home to enjoy the scenery and the peace and quiet. Slow jams played quietly from the radio as I cruised down I-95. I took in the city lights as I made my way home. It took me no time since there were hardly any cars out. When I entered my home, I smelled the familiar exotic scent mixed with what smelled like Puerto Rican food. Walking to the fridge I found several food containers and my favorite beer. A small smile formed on my face. I reset the alarm and jogged up the stairs. The site before me had me grinning from ear to ear which is normally out of character for me unless I'm with my son.

Julissa was asleep in my bed with the covers pulled almost completely over her head. After I showered and slipped on some boxers I climbed in next to her then softly kissed her on the lips. She stirred and blinked until her eyes opened; she grinned.

"Did you have fun? I heard from Lauryn that you and Eric were out." I kissed her cheek and nipped the side of her neck with my teeth. She giggled then moaned.

"This what the two of you are going to be doing? Sharing our location with each other?"

"No, you know better than that. I was telling her that I was going to surprise you with dinner and she mentioned that you might not have made it in yet."

She tried to sit up in the bed and I pushed her back down.

"Nah, slow your roll. Ain't nobody trying to have long, in-depth conversations tonight. Ya man is tired."

Julissa smirked and gripped me from under the covers before she worked her way under them.

"Too tired for this?"

Laying my head back onto the pillow and bit my lip to stop from groaning. No doubt she had my approval. "Never that baby."

JULISSA

T hankfully, I was able to find a small office space that would be perfect for my company. Brandon wanted to purchase property for me, but I was serious when I told him that I wanted to do this on my own, so I was renting an office in one of those cool shared space office buildings near downtown. With it came with a lot of cool amenities such as a café and library. I loved it. The office was quiet, and I was focused on finishing these event invitations that I'd been working on. The client had been extremely specific about what they wanted and there was no way that I wouldn't deliver. Gently Richards was a popular philanthropist and community advocate and she ran a non-profit that served girls from the inner city. They were having their annual empowerment tea which brought out the who's who of South Florida. She found me on social media, love my work and the rest was history. I'd woken up at the crack of dawn and left Brandon lying peacefully in bed. His massive frame usually took over my entire bed and you could find me somewhere curled up under him. Brandon preferred that I slept at his place since he had a massive California King bed. He didn't even move when I slid from under his protective hold. He tended to hold me as if someone would break in and try to take me. The thought made a smirk form across my face as I sipped my green jasmine tea, the warmth of it coated my throat and relaxed me.

I liked getting to the office space early before my assistants arrive because once they did it would be with a barrage of questions or random conversations. I worked better in silence with maybe just a little mood music turned down low. My coconut, vanilla, and tuberose candles had my office smelling sensually sweet. The lights were off with the exception of my desk lamp and the candlelight. I only needed to tweak the metallic rose gold on the invitation and I could move on to my next project. There was a light tap at the door that made me jump. I looked up to see Draya, one of my assistants poke her head in. Draya's smile could disarm a damn terrorist. As much as I wanted to tell her to scram, I went ahead and waved her in.

"Hey boss lady." She drawled in her southern accent.

"Hi Draya! What's up?"

"Nothing much. Just thought I get an early start today. I'm surprised to see you here."

"Yeah I'm here more early mornings than you know but I just wanted to finish up the invites for the tea and fundraiser. I promised that all corrections would be made by tomorrow. I also want to spend the rest of the day having some me time."

"Okay! I ain't mad at that. Do you need anything?"

"Nope, I'm good. How's that book cover going?" Draya's eyes lit up and she walked closer to my desk.

"It's going great! Ms. Lauryn has been a huge help and I am learning a lot. I realized that there was a lot that I didn't know, but Lauryn's brain is like... Google!" Lauryn agreed to mentor Draya and teach her how to design book and magazine covers. She worked with her weekly to check-in and give feedback.

"O-kay... Great! I knew you two would work well together. Lauryn is a fantastic teacher, but enough talking. I need to finish this and be about my business."

"Right." Draya laughed and made her way out of the office. "I'll see you later Ms. Julissa!"

After a couple of hours. I felt good about my work and passed it on to Megan, my other assistant, for printing and packaging. When I entered my unit, I was engulfed with the smell of bacon and what was probably chicken and waffles, my favorite.

"Brandon?"

"Yo!"

I sauntered into the kitchen and placed my hand on my hip. His head bobbed to the music he was playing.

"What are you up to in here?"

"What does it look like?"

So, I was interacting with the *smart-ass* Brandon this morning. With a roll of my eyes I sucked my teeth and spun around. When his strong arms wrapped me up in a bear hug from behind, I bit my lip to hide the look of victory on my face. Full soft lips pressed into my cheek close to the corner of my mouth.

"Stop being a brat JuJu bean. It's obvious that I'm making breakfast. I figured you would be back soon since you snuck out of bed so damn early."

"Sorry, I was trying not to wake you." I spun around, wrapped my arms around his neck and kissed him on the lips. He donned a lazy grin and held my waist. He tasted like orange juice and weed.

"That won't ever happen baby. I sleep light."

"I know but you looked like you were knocked out." Brandon pecked me on the nose and walked back towards the stove. Brandon was practically naked, cooking only in his boxer briefs that hugged his strong thighs perfectly. His huge, beefy, tatted chest on full display. It was a sight to behold. I leaned against the counter and enjoyed the view. He spoke while he moved around my kitchen with familiarity.

"Don't get it twisted I was sleeping good as hell, but the moment you left my arms, I was up."

Brandon worked to quickly plate our food while I gazed upon him in wonder. He could say and do the sweetest things and not even realize it. My mouth watered in anticipation of breakfast. I'd only had two cups of green tea since I woke up earlier and was famished. Brandon was a great cook. He'd taught himself at a young age when he realized that he could not depend on his mother or family to see that he had at least three decent meals a day. Grams, Eric's grandmother took time to teach him and Eric when she eventually took him in. By the time he was seventeen he was living on his own. He'd grown up too fast. Loosing Grams affected him more than he showed but he would always take a seat back to Eric's feelings when it came to her. Lucky for him, Eric was a great friend and understood that Brandon had suffered a lost too.

"Baby, you're drooling." I looked up and he was smirking at me. *Arrogant ass.*

"Whatever. I was not drooling."

I stopped ogling my man long enough to set the table and pour our drinks. We sat across from each other. When Brandon grasped both of my hands and bowed his head to pray, I smiled and followed along.

"Father, we thank you. Thank you for second chances and continuous mercy. Amen."

When I raised my head, his eyes were on me and I blushed. "Amen."

Not dwelling on the sweet moment for too long, we dove into our food. Brandon's plate held twice the amount of food as mine, maybe more. I slowly chewed my waffle and enjoyed the decadent sweet buttery red velvet flavor. The wings were fried perfectly; everything was good. I wiped my mouth and took a sip of my orange juice.

"Baby, this is delicious." Brandon simply grunted some inaudible response and kept shoveling food into his mouth. He preferred not to talk while eating. I still carried on a conversation since I knew he was listening. I shared how my morning went and my excitement for my growing graphic design company. As I finished off my last piece of bacon Brandon's phone rang. He looked at his phone and quickly cleaned his hands before picking up.

"Jay what's up?" My eyes left my plate and landed on his face. All I could get was a few head nods and cave man sounds and he picked up for *her.* I tried to rationalize that she was the mother of his child and it could be an emergency but it would be a lie if I said that his actions didn't sting. I shot up from my seat and grabbed my plate and his unfinished plate. I raked his food in the garbage and tossed the dishes in the dish washer. He was still on the phone but followed my every move with his eyes. He was incensed.

"Yeah I can get him from school tomorrow. We'll hang out before I take him home. Yeah. Bye."

My heart pounded in my chest as I watched him push back from the table. I cringed at the sound of the chair scratching the hardwood floor. He was on me in seconds. I tried to put on a brave face but Brandon could be intimidating at times.

"Yo what the fuck is wrong with you?"

"First, watch how you talk to me. Second, what was that shit? I can't get one word out of you and then she called and... Move Brandon." His hand cradled my chin so that I would look at him.

"We agreed to start over, right?"

When I didn't respond and attempted to walk past him he stood in my way and bent over into my face. "Right?"

"Yes! What you just did just brought up... You know what, forget it. I'm entitled to my feelings, but I shouldn't take them out on you. I'm tripping."

"Julissa when did you become jealous of Jaynah?"

"When she became the mother of you first child and gave you a boy. When you admitted that you started back fucking her after we broke up." I responded barely above a whisper. That got him up off of me. He held his hands up in surrender.

"Alright, that's fair. Come here."

Brandon lead me to the couch, sat down and pulled me down on his lap. He didn't say anything right away so I knew that he was in his head. He didn't talk much but when he did, he always wanted his words to be meaningful. I rubbed his head and massaged the back of his neck. When we were this close, I couldn't help but touch him.

"I talked to Jay about me and you getting back together and set some expectations regarding her actions. I hope that I don't have to do that with you. I hadn't planned on it. What I am about to say to you I'm only going to say this once Ju and you can do what you want with it. I don't want Jay. I'm not in love with her and I don't have any lingering feelings for her. She's the mother of my son so I do love her, but like I love family. I'm going to have to answer her calls; she has my son the majority of the time. His safety and well-being is a priority, but also I won't let her use that to cause drama. What I am trying to build with you, I will never jeopardize. I won't ever betray your trust. If I wasn't clear then here it is. You are it for me Julissa. I come home to you or to my spot alone. Do we have an understanding?"

Slowly, I nodded my head. I couldn't find the words to respond. He smiled at my stuttering and kissed me.

"Baby I need you to say it."

I sighed. "I hear you and I understand. I guess I just need to work on some things on my end. You used this time apart to work on yours and I held on to resentment and pain. I'm sorry."

"No, I'm sorry I caused that shit, but ya man ain't going nowhere Puerto Rican princess."

I tossed my head back and laughed. "Are you ever going to stop calling me that?"

"Nah. Now let me get up in them guts real quick before I go to the office."

"Brandon!"

Tweddle Dum: How long are you going to ignore your family. We are your real family, not them!

My family, with the exception of my dad, were constantly calling and texting me, my older sister more than others. I wasn't ready to talk to them and my sister's recent text let me know that shit ain't change. I couldn't go without responding.

Me: Who is them? Lauryn? My friends who have always supported me no matter what? The people who are there for me when you are not? You can go somewhere with that. What's wrong? No one to transfer your feelings to because you regret marrying your boring ass husband?

That was a bitch move but I knew that would get her off my back for a couple of weeks. I had to deal with my family when I was ready, not on their terms.

"Who is that? Brandon?"

"No. Just Amara trying to pull me back into their fold."

"Oh." Lauryn busied herself with the care packages we were putting together. Every year we sponsored a local housing program for women or mothers and created care packages for them. We also hold an annual diaper drive to give to programs in need. Every so often she would glance at me. Tired of her nonverbal messages I huffed and turned my attention to her.

"What Lauryn?"

"What do you mean? I'm working." She tried to look nonchalant and busy herself with the boxes.

"Yeah, but your silence is loud as hell. Come on Chica. Spit it out."

"It's nothing." I waited. She turned around and shook her head.

"They're your family Ju and at the end of the day some messed up shit was said but they are good people. They love you."

"I need their respect and for them to show their love. Putting me down is not displaying love." I shook my head.

"I know but..."

"No buts Lauryn."

"Look you know how I am about family. Everyday ain't promise. Don't let this feud go on for too long. That's all."

I didn't respond and instead went back to the job at hand. Together we packed up twenty-five boxes filled with toiletries and goodies. This was a labor of love for us. We always said that once we got settled in our careers that we would find a way to give back, so we created a non-profit called Thankful Blessings. Right now, it was just the two of us, but we were looking into grants to allow us to expand. Eric offered to fund it, but Lauryn wanted us to do this on our own. My phone alerted that I had a new text message. I smiled assuming that it was Brandon.

Ethan: Hey, can we meet up and talk?

Ethan had called me a few times after Brandon bulldozed through our date. I was hoping that he would get the hint and move on, but he obviously needed some type of closure. He hadn't done anything wrong so I could give him that.

Me: Okay. When?

"Are you mad at me?" Even though she was about to be a mother of two and could be a pit bull in a skirt, Lauryn was still sensitive as hell. I smiled and threw tissue paper at her ass.

"No, I'm not mad at you. I'm just contemplating."

"Okay. You know that anything I say to you is always out of love, right?"

"Yes, I know and I heard you. Trust."

"Cool. Plus, I miss your mom's cooking."

"Heffa!" I tossed more tissue paper at her. We both laughed as we stacked the boxes and cleaned up Lauryn's Project Room that Eric surprised her with. He was tired of seeing evidence of her projects all over the house, so he enlisted me in redesigning one of the guest bedrooms downstairs.

"Shit! I gotta pick up Kin from my parents' house. Are you staying for dinner? You want to ride with me?"

"Sure! I'm sure Mrs. T has some type of bomb ass pie on display in the kitchen."

JULISSA

B randon and I had been going strong for a couple of months now and I couldn't be happier. If I wasn't at work or hanging with my best friends, then I was with Brandon. We were learning things about each other every day. For example, I had no idea that he knew how to actually date. When we first got together before BJ, we spent most of our time indoors, unless Lauryn and I planned a double date. Now, instead of me always suggesting that we get out the house, Brandon was purposeful in planning dates. My favorite one was when he surprised me with a weekend trip to the Bahamas. He'd chartered a yacht that was equipped like an apartment; there was no need to rent a hotel for the weekend. We explored the area, rode jet skis, swam in the beautiful ocean, ate, danced, and sexed each other damn near into delirium. While there, he surprised me with the opportunity to go snorkeling, which was something that I'd been dying to do. When I returned to work on Monday my staff couldn't stop pointing out how I was so relaxed for a Monday. I only smiled and told them that I had a great weekend. That following weekend we all celebrated BJ's third birthday together without a hitch. Well, Jaynah ignored me like I wasn't there but other than that his celebration was a success and he had so much fun being the center of attention. He got that trait from his mama.

Even with all the good that was happening I couldn't let go of the fear of losing apart of myself. Brandon and I were opposites in more ways than I could count. We liked different things and where I was spontaneous and open to new experiences, Brandon was stubborn and set in his ways. He did what he could but some days I needed more. If I was honest with myself, I needed space. I'd been spending more of my time at his place since I felt bad about him having to sleep in my bed that was obviously too small for him. I'm fit but I'm still a thick chick so both of us sharing a queen bed wasn't cutting it. I was even spending more time with him and BJ without all the drama from Jaynah, which was a relief. My mom used to always tell me that no matter what I would never be satisfied because I always wanted more. *Well, duh.* What was wrong with wanting more? I just needed to find time to do the things that I liked.

"Earth to boss lady, earth to boss lady."

"Huh? What?" I blinked and noticed the ring filled hand waving in my face. Both Draya and Megan were staring at me in amusement. Draya laughed.

"Yo, where did you go?"

"And with who?" Megan added. She wiggled her eyebrows.

"Shit, I'm sorry I was just… Never mind."

"Uh huh. You were thinking about that big ol' handsome man that came in here the other day to escort you to lunch. No disrespect but that man was built by the gods. Damn Ms. Ju!"

I laughed and scribbled something down on my iPad. "Alright Meg, but he is fine and he is all mine."

"I usually don't like men that big but… never mind." We all giggled and I could tell that the girls wanted to dive deeper about Brandon and ask the question that all of my friends had asked with the exception of Lauryn. It was an answer I would never give, and women would have to keep on guessing because I don't want anyone trying to test if what I shared was true.

"Exactly. I don't kiss and tell. Let's get back down to business." We were interrupted when a delivery man entered the suite carrying a beautiful arrangement of peonies. My two assistants gasped and bounced in excitement.

"Julissa Rivera?"

"Um that's me. My face flushed and I rubbed my cheeks before reaching out for the fancy bouquet."

"Oh wow! Is that from snack ministry bae?" I narrowed my eyes at Megan to issue her a silent warning before opening the card.

Just wanted to say thanks- Ethan

Fuck. I tucked the card into my pocket and put on my best smile. These weren't from Brandon and there was no way I could bring them home so I placed them in the middle of the small conference room table for everyone to enjoy. My phone rang and Ethan's name displayed on the screen. I dismissed the girls, headed into my office and plopped down in my chair.

"Hi Ethan."

"What's up? Did you like your surprise?"

"Um... I did. They're beautiful; breathtaking. Thank you. You didn't have to."

"Yeah I did. You didn't have to meet up with me and I appreciate that you did. Like I said, I would still like to be friends with you."

"Even after you met my now crazy boyfriend?" I smirked and crossed my legs.

"Yeah. I can't blame him for what happened. The thought of losing a woman like you should drive any man insane. Anyway, I don't want to take too much of your time but I have another event next week and I would love for you to come."

Say no, say no, say no. "Sure! Just let me know where." *What am I saying?*

"Good. I'll text you the details and you're more than welcome to bring your bodyguard."

"Ethan..."

"I'm joking. Your boyfriend is more than welcomed to come."

"Okay Ethan, but I have to get back to work."

"Yeah, of course. So, I'll talk to you later."

"Okay. Bye."

I smiled at the picture of Brandon and I on my home screen that we took at the beach. He was wearing shades and a hat. His dimples were on full display as he towered over me from behind. When I wasn't with Brandon, which was now most of the time,

I was with Lauryn, Monica, or working. A little change wouldn't hurt. There was an annoying voice in my head that was telling me that I should separate myself from Ethan but I knew that my heart was with Brandon, so what harm could it do?

BIZZIE

There were days when I wished that I was back in the streets. The street life came easy to me. Fuck that, the money came easy. Entering the business world was slightly harder than I expected and I don't mean hard as in I couldn't do it, but hard as in the number of hours in the day that I had to put in to ensure the steady flow of income that I was used to. Owning property and businesses took up a lot of my time and I now had to be mindful of how I spent it. I was no longer a solo act. My days were carefully planned out to devote quality time to my son and accommodate my relationship with Julissa. I was working on building wealth and I wanted BJ to have all the opportunities in the world to do and be whatever he wanted. It was my goal to leave a legacy of wealth that would take care of my lineage.

I grew up in a shitty ass family who didn't give a damn about me. My family didn't know anything about love, which was why I was so hesitant when I found out that Jaynah was pregnant. I knew how to protect and be loyal, but I wasn't sure if I knew how to love. I was afraid that I wasn't capable of loving a kid but the moment my son made his arrival my heart quadrupled, and I finally understood the meaning of unconditional love. I also finally understood that there was something incredibly wrong with the people I shared DNA with because they were incapable of love.

My day had been long. I'd gotten up early to hit the gym before I met up with my realtor to look at some properties. After that I went over to my office and the club and looked over financial reports with my bookkeeper. Eric wanted to go over some changes to the lounge so him, Kevin, and I met up for a lunch meeting that turned into us hanging out afterwards. Just as I stepped outside from the lounge Jaynah hit me up asking if I could take BJ for the night since she was pulling a double, so I headed on over to pick him up. When I entered his classroom, his face lit up and he ran into my arms. I apologized to the teacher for being late then me and my little man headed home.

Once we made it home, I got BJ settled in front of the TV and started on his favorite dinner, spaghetti and meatballs. It wasn't until then that I realized that I hadn't heard from Julissa all day which was strange. She was always texting me some motivational shit or sharing something she found interesting or funny. I checked the time and it was already going on six in the evening so I decided to hit her up.

"Hey."

"Hey? That's all you got? Where are you?" She sighed then sucked her teeth.

"I'm outside Brandon. Don't tell me I have to check in now."

The alarm alerted letting me know that the front door was opened. The clack of heels grew louder as Julissa entered the kitchen and family room. She didn't smile when she stretched up on her toes to kiss me. Her hair was wild and her face was free of makeup. I held her at arm's length and studied her pulse as I rubbed my thumbs over her inner wrist.

"You better had brought that fine ass over here. You look tired." She didn't respond and opted to join my son on the floor in front of the TV instead. She scooped him up and planted kisses on both cheeks then his forehead before she sat on the floor and placed him on her lap. We ate dinner in silence so I was surprised when she helped me bathe BJ and get him ready for bed. I was over her moodiness so once we were in the bedroom, I addressed her.

"Yo! What is up with you today?"

"Huh? What?" She avoided eye contact. That move didn't sit well with me.

"You've been distracted and moody since you got here and I ain't hear from you all day. What the hell is wrong with you?"

"Am I not allowed to have an off day? Can you give me that?"

"You can have an off day but damn, say something. You can't just go ghost on me physically or emotionally." A smile threatened to form on her face.

"Today was super busy and tiring. That is all. You missed me?"

"What do you think?"

"That's just it Brandon. It's only been a few hours and you are…"

"IT'S BEEN ALL DAMN DAY!" I hollered. She sighed and rolled her neck.

"It's been a few hours and you are tripping!"

"We are in a relationship and people who are in a relationship check in with each other. When I want something, I don't hold back Ju. I'm all in and I need you to be all in."

"Where were you when I was ready? You weren't there! You were with… her." She croaked. Her bottom lip trembled, and she tried to hide it by pulling it in between her teeth. "Brandon I am trying. You're not being fair. I agreed to give this another shot, but I'll be damned if I let you bully me into rushing this!"

"Julissa…"

"No! Let me finish. I am here, Brandon. As much as it scares me and as much as I am tempted to give in to my natural inclination and run, I am committed to you. Just chill the fuck out. Please." She dropped down on the bed and exhaled. She looked like she just got a load off of her chest. Maybe I was pushing too much.

"Damn, my bad baby. We just lost so much time and… shit I don't know. There ain't that many people that I'm close to and we've always had this vibe since I first met you. I was immediately drawn to your perky, bubbly ass. You were just too damn happy and full of energy. Also, I thought you were sexy as fuck. I've never felt this way Ju and I don't want to lose this feeling again. I don't want to lose you." Julissa stood back up and wrapped her arms around my waist. That simple gesture, along with the smell of her exotic perfume, had me bricking up.

"Babe. Let's just enjoy each other and allow whatever is happening between us to progress naturally. No pressure."

"Yeah, I can do that because this shit is intense as fuck." I dipped down and kissed her neck then pulled her even closer to my throbbing erection. She moaned.

"What I feel for you is intense as fuck."

I began to undress. Julissa followed my lead. Once we were both completely naked I scooped her up and entered her slowly. She hissed as she adjusted to my size. Her warmth surrounding me felt so damn good that I already knew this first round would be quick. I pressed her back into the wall and stroked her long and hard until we both came and her essence coated my length. Round two was slow and deliberate as I took my time pleasing every part of her body and she did the same. Our love making was intense and our moans and grunts filled the room until we both had nothing left. After we washed up, she snuggled up next to me and held on like she was afraid that I would leave. There was something off about her today; something she wasn't telling me and I couldn't put my finger on it. I wouldn't press the issue anymore today, but I was definitely going to keep my eye on her. I never had to question Julissa before so I didn't like what I was feeling.

JULISSA

I stepped into the restaurant and looked around for any sign of my girls. High pitched laughter led me towards the back where there weren't that many people seated. Monica and Lauryn were smiling and sipping from glasses decorated with fancy fruit and edible decorations. It was good to see the two of them getting along. Somedays they were hot and cold.

"Hey. What's so funny?" I took my seat and browsed the drink menu. When the waitress stopped by, I ordered a passion fruit Caipirinha.

"Nothing really. Just strolling down memory lane and Lauryn was updating me on the *joys* of motherhood."

Monica's last statement was laced with sarcasm. She swore she was never having children and couldn't believe Lauryn was going on two. Her last breakup had really changed her outlook on love. She dated but no one ever got to a third date.

"Oh. So, what's knew with you Mo?" I placed my elbows on the table and propped my chin on my hands.

"Well let's see, I take my licensure exam in two weeks. If I pass then I will be on my way to opening up my spa. I built a good relationship with the people I worked on while in school, so I already have a few clients who are willing to help get the word out."

"And you have us," Lauryn assured.

"Definitely. We can talk about creating flyers, a website, and branding. We got you!"

"I know. It feels good to have the old crew back together again.

I miss you two!"

"Yeah it does feel good," Lauryn agreed.

"I'm glad I was finally able to get you two out at the same time. Y'all was wearing me out!"

"Speaking of the crew back together; Lauryn why aren't you going out with us tonight? Can't Eric watch the babies so you can have the night off?" I tried my best to get Monica's attention by clearing my throat and kicking her under the table, but she was oblivious.

"Umm. I have no idea what you're talking about." Lauryn tilted her head towards me. Her eyes were filled with questions. I felt like a child that was about to get in trouble.

"We're going to the B-Side Lounge to see that fine ass poet." Monica fell back in her chair as she fanned herself. She took a sip of her water.

"What? Ethan?" Lauryn looked at me like I had an extra titty. "Ju..."

"Lauryn it's fine. We're friends." I waved her off.

"The hell you are, and it is not fine. You and that man use to bang it out. There is no way that you can be friends with him. More important than that, Brandon will lose his shit! I know you don't think that Eric was out in the streets being crazy by himself."

"He will be fine because I'm not doing anything wrong."

"Does he know?"

"Huh?" My eyes focused on my drink as I occupied myself with stirring it with my straw.

"Does Brandon know?"

"I mean no, but..."

"Dammit Julissa. You said that you wanted your relationship to work. This ain't the way to do it sis. You are playing with fire." Monica looked between Lauryn and I like she was watching a tennis match.

"Look, I know what I'm doing. I have it under control. If it makes you feel any better, I'll tell him tomorrow. Don't worry."

"Tomorrow?! Okay Ju, do you. But I am warning you, if Brandon finds out on his own, I can't deny that his reaction will be anything but rational. Bro is not wrapped too tight."

Lauryn flagged the waitress back to the table and we all gave our individual orders. I knew she was worried, but I needed my friend to trust me. Things with Brandon and I were progressing fast and I just needed to feel a little bit of freedom before diving all the way in. It would be fine. Just one last meetup with Ethan and I would let him know that we couldn't be friends anymore. Plus, Monica would be there. Everything was good.

• •

After looking towards the entrance for the umpteenth time, I had to laugh at myself. Lauryn had me a little paranoid. I knew I was wrong for hanging out with Ethan behind Brandon's back, but it was totally innocent. Lauryn and I used to hit up this poetry lounge way before I met Ethan so what was the difference in me accepting his invites compared to me going on my own? Anyway, his invite included free admission and VIP treatment; that definitely didn't hurt. We'd hung out one other time since he first invited me to his show, and I was once again hanging out in VIP seating waiting for him to perform. Monica was supposed to join me, but she bailed out at the last minute. It made me wonder if Lauryn had gotten to her. Before we left the restaurant earlier, she did not hesitate to rip into me. I wasn't surprised she was in her head for the remainder of lunch; she just couldn't help herself. She told me that I was playing with fire and was going to lose Brandon, but I told her that she was exaggerating. Now I was doubting my decision.

The place was crowded tonight but that was to be expected. Ethan was a local favorite and was specifically a favorite with the ladies. When he stepped to the mic the room erupted with cheers and screams from admires. Ethan flashed his signature smile and adjusted the mic. The lights dimmed and everyone quieted. As the music played and he spoke his first word he had the crowd captivated, including me. His voice was smooth and sultry. He was skilled at switching up the tone and cadence of his voice to make you feel his words. When his eyes found me, he winked and bit his bottom lip, playing into the vibe he was creating. I raised my wine glass and smiled.

After his set, he made his way over to my table. I clapped my hands and giggled.

"Great job Ethan *the Poet*. You were amazing as usual." He placed his arm around me and placed a kiss on my cheek. His lips remained on my face long enough for me to eye him with suspicion. but not long enough to be inappropriate.

"Thank you, thank you. Are you enjoying yourself? Have they been treating you well?"

"Uh yeah. The service has been great. Thank you for the special treatment."

"You are special Ju. What happened to...?"

"Brandon. That's his name. Poetry isn't really his thing. It's more of something my best friend and I have in common."

"And me." Ethan's fingers gently grazed mine. My breathing seized and I cleared my throat. I sipped my wine to give a reason to pull my hand away.

"What?"

"I understand your love for poetry." The look in Ethan's eyes said everything that I convinced myself wasn't the case. He still wanted me. Hell, he wanted me now. Sex with Ethan was different but also the type of experience you had to share with your best friend and I found my body reacting to the memory. This was wrong.

"I understand a lot about you, Julissa. You don't have to commit to one person right now. You're still young. I know you're not ready to be lock down. We were having fun..."

"Ethan..."

"Ah hell. I know that face. Seriously? The friend zone already?" He leaned back in his seat and held his arms out.

I shrugged and smirked. "I'm in love. I love him and I think that he's the one for me."

"Wow. Well, okay. I- I guess I wish you the best. I can't say that I am happy for you because that would be a lie. I do hope that he makes you happy and if he doesn't then you have my number."

At that statement, I tossed my head back and laughed. Ethan leaned in and pecked me on the cheek before bidding me farewell and walking away. I released a sigh of relief. I'd just dodged a bullet.

BIZZIE

When she allowed him to step into her space and kiss her on the cheek I immediately saw red. I was moving before I could fully process the interaction that I witnessed between the two of them. My legs made a beeline towards that nigga. As soon as I received a photo from Jay that included Julissa at the lounge where he was performing tonight, I knew her ass was up to no good. I knew that Jay was being messy, but she was no longer my problem. Julissa was. Nah, Ethan was.

"BRANDON NO! Brandon! Stop! Please stop. Oh my God Brandon please!"

There were several hands on me attempting to pull me off of that nigga. I couldn't hear shit, just the ringing in my ears. A shock to my body caused me to release him as my entire body went stiff and convulsed. My hearing came back in a snap and I could hear Julissa's screams and what sounded like chaos.

"What are you doing? Stop! You're going to kill him!" I looked up to see Ju being manhandled by a cop. I was handcuffed before I could react. When she was slammed on the ground next to me I damn near broke my wrist trying to break free.

"You a dumb ass muthafucka for that! I am going to..."

"Brandon no!" My eyes landed on Ju and she shook her head. Unshed tears rimmed her eyes. I was yanked by my arms until I stood up. Julissa was being walked outside by a female cop and an EMT was looking over Ethan. Before I could see where Ju was, I was shoved in the back of a squad car and carried off.

Once I was booked, I was placed in a holding cell. I took a seat in a corner and rested my head on the wall. To say I was pissed was an understatement. I could kill five niggas with my bare hands right about now. This whole night had me questioning everything about Ju and if I ever really knew her. Shit, maybe I just ignored the damn signs. I hadn't spent a night in jail since Eric and I got caught riding around in a stolen car when we were about sixteen. We both made a promise that we would never go back to jail but I guess we both broke that promise. This was going to be a long fucking night. I was simply glad that this shit didn't happen on the weekend.

JULISSA

"**H**ey bestie!"

"Lauryn!" I shrieked.

"What! What happened? Hello? JULISSA!"

"It's Brandon. He was just arrested. He got in a fight at the B-Side Lounge." Lauryn's end of the line was so quiet that I pulled the phone away from my ear to see if she was still there.

"Hello? Lauryn."

"Who was he fighting Julissa?" Her tone was clipped. Here she go with the authoritative tone like she was my elder. This was what I didn't have time for. I didn't call my best friend to be chastised like a child. I already knew I messed up.

"Look Lauryn I didn't call you for a lecture. If that's what you are on, then I'll just hang up and call Eric."

"Julissa you have some nerve! You know what? We don't have time for this." She stopped speaking and I could hear her and Eric talking. When Eric's voice boomed with a "*What the fuck!*" I jumped. I'd witness Eric in his element and it could be scary.

"Ju! You're on speaker phone and you better start talking now." Eric growled on the other end of the line. My first instinct was to check him for speaking to me in that manner but getting Brandon out of jail was more important. With a shaky voice I explained everything that went down. Unbeknownst to Brandon there were cops that had already pulled up to the lounge to handle a rowdy customer who was pissy drunk at the bar.

Outside of the jail I paced back and forth while I waited for Eric and Lauryn to show up. Brandon was able to post bail and they were coming from meeting with a bondsman. Sleeping alone the night before was damn near impossible and Brandon's presence was missed. It just felt so wrong. I looked up to see them strutting through the parking lot. When they were upon me I held my breath. They didn't say much to me at the courthouse, so I knew they were both still stewing in their anger. Lauryn snatched her arm from Eric and approached me. Eric narrowed his eyes at the both of us and entered the building.

"WHAT WERE YOU THINKING?" My neck snapped back. Lauryn and I had fights but she had never yelled at me like that. This was unexpected.

"I, I didn't..."

"You're right you didn't think. They tased him Ju! This could have ended badly. He could have been killed! What did you think Bizzie would do if he found out you were friends with Ethan?"

"Wait. Who the hell do you think you're talking to? Don't fucking yell at me! He only wanted to hang out as friends Lauryn. Is it a crime to have a guy friend?"

"If you fucked him before, yes!"

"Oh, so it's okay when you do it because the both of you are buddy, buddy with Kevin."

"Whatever Ju. That shit didn't happen until Kevin and I were over each other. We were friends first *and* he would never invite me somewhere without making sure Eric was coming. What you did was shady and sneaky. *That's* the difference!" We were at a standoff and neither one of us was willing to back down.

"Ladies." Eric cleared his throat to get our attention. I spun around in time to see Brandon push through the revolving doors. His nose was flared and there was tension in his jaw. When his eyes landed on me his body stiffened, but he recovered fast. I tried my best to put on a brave face and smiled as he approached me. When he brushed past me, my face fell and my spirit was crushed. I opened my mouth to speak but he tossed his hand up to stop me.

"Don't say shit. I need a break from you; can't even look at your ass," he growled.

"A break? What do you mean a break?" He shook his head and unleased a sinister laugh. Eric stepped in between us.

"Come on let's go. We don't want to draw no attention. Y'all can hash this shit out in privacy."

"Bet. Can y'all drop me off?" I side stepped Eric and stood chest to chest with Brandon.

"Are you serious Brandon?"

"As a heart attack. You don't want to be alone in a small enclosed space with me right now."

With that he just walked off with our friends. I felt alone and misunderstood. My first thought was to take my ass home but I needed to put on my big girl panties and work this out with Brandon, so I headed to his place. When I pulled up he was just getting out of Eric's truck. He held the front door open for me to walk in first. The door slammed and I jumped. He stormed off into the living room and I dragged behind after hanging up my purse.

"You're not sure about this. You can't be and now I'm not sure about you. I have a son Ju! BJ needs me and I can't do shit for him if I'm dead or locked the fuck up!"

"I know that and I am so sorry. I never wanted…"

"Do you think this is a damn game Ju? I thought you wanted this."

"I do, but I don't want to get hurt." Brandon took a step back. Underneath the rage I saw pain.

"You still think that I would hurt you?"

I looked down at the ground and ran my hand through my messy hair. "I don't know."

"I LOVE YOU! When will you fucking get it? I've never loved another woman in this way."

Our eyes met and he looked crushed. That broke me to see him so raw. Tears ran down my face. Things were going so well between us and I couldn't believe that things had took a turn for the worse. Brandon made his way towards the stairs.

"Baby wait. Please don't walk away."

"Look Ju, I don't have time to be putting energy into a relationship that your indecisive ass is unsure about. I had a long night, I need to wash my ass, and I'm tired. You can sit here and figure out what you want but I'm taking my ass to bed. This is some bullshit."

I stood in the living room with my mouth gaped open as Brandon stomped up the stairs. You could cut the tension in the air with a knife and I didn't know if I should stay or leave. I paced back and forth in the entry way trying to figure out my next move. Leaving would prove him right and he would probably assume that I didn't really want to be in a serious relationship. Running when things got rough was my M.O. I didn't like conflict and drama. What I really wanted to do was to call Lauryn to help me figure this out, but she was obviously infuriated with me. As is if she could feel my thoughts a text message came in.

Lauryn: Your ass better stay and work that shit out. I'm not playing!

Me: He is so enraged right now. I don't know what to do.

Lauryn: Give him a little space. Do not sleep in a guest room, get your ass in the bed with him and apologize again.

Lauryn: And Eric is mad at me because I knew what you were up to.

Me: I'm sorry. I can talk to him.

Lauryn: Terrible idea. He's mad at you too. Don't worry. He'll be okay once I give him some. Lol. Call me tomorrow. Love you.

Me: Okay. Love you too.

Since Brandon locked me out of the room. I busied myself with texting Monica, watching movies, and doing some online shopping. Once I was bored with that, I ventured out back and lounged by the pool. Droplets of water splashed on my face and I jumped up from my peaceful slumber. I hadn't realized I fell asleep. I made a mad dash into the house before the rain came pouring down. After a quick glance at the time I realized that it was after six in the evening and that was when the thought crossed my mind that Brandon hadn't eaten since sometime the day before. Him coming to the lounge meant that he most likely hadn't eaten dinner yet. He had to be hungry and his stubborn ass probably planned to stay locked up in the room. Nah, he didn't have an avoidant personality. He would come to the kitchen to cook, but just ignore me until he was ready to speak. Something told me that I would be closer to losing him if I didn't make some sort of gesture tonight.

With a huff I pulled the sliding glass door closed and made my way into the kitchen to whip up some burgers and fries. I placed a couple of beers in the freezer so that they would be nice and chilled for Brandon. If he didn't want to speak to me, I knew the smell of food would at least draw him out. Just as I was finishing up his burger and placing a healthy serving of fries on his plate I heard heavy feet making their way down the stairs. His clean masculine scent teased my senses. I inhaled and quietly moaned. When my eyes opened Brandon stood towering over me. His expression held indifference.

"Hey! Um, I thought you needed to eat after… Well anyway I made you a burger and fries."

"Thanks." He lifted the plate from my hand and sat at the counter. I placed one of the beers in the fridge and sat one in front of him. I fixed my plate then sat next to him. We ate in silence. I would love to say the silence was comfortable but it wasn't. One thing about Brandon was that he could be feeling murderous yet his expression would remain emotionless; like he had a switch to shut them off. That was the treatment that I was getting. I couldn't take it.

"Brandon I'm sorry." Instead of responding he took a huge bite of his sandwich and stuffed a handful of fries in his mouth. I patiently waited for a response that never came; my temper was starting to flare.

"Do you want me here?" Nothing. "If you are going to just give me the silent treatment then I can leave." Brandon shot up from his seat and tossed his plate in the sink. The loud crash of the dish told me it shattered. Before I could blink, he was in my face and wearing a scowl on his.

"Then go Ju. Ain't nobody begging you to be here right now. Go check on ya boy."

My bottom lip trembled but tears wouldn't help my case, so

I swallowed them back. I had no right to cry. I hadn't spent the night in jail after seeing my significant other with someone else.

"Brandon stop!" I pleaded with him.

"Stop talking to me Ju. I don't want to hear your voice right now!" He damn near barked at me before he made his way back upstairs. I swallowed the lump in my throat then proceeded to clean up the kitchen. After a quick shower I climbed in the bed with Brandon and for the first time ever we slept on separate sides of the bed.

BIZZIE

Over a week had past and I hadn't said much to Julissa other than a few one-word responses to her many questions and eventually she stopped trying, but she was still here. She hadn't left. I'd forgiven her days ago, but she needed to learn that you couldn't make mistakes and expect people to get over it just because you say that you are sorry. She needed to know that she fucked up. I wanted to make sure that she never pulled no shit like that again or she would find herself single again. It was apparent that she was just buying her time before I completely broke things off, but I had no intentions of doing that. I just didn't know how to get us back to how things were.

My lawyer had reached out to let me know that although I'd fucked Ethan up, he'd refused to press charges. I hate to admit it but that made me feel like shit for beating his ass. He deserved it because I knew Ju told him about me, but I knew he was no match for me. I had my lawyer to get his statement in writing and sent a check over that would cover his hospital bill and then some. I was grateful that I didn't have to deal with going to court and spending more time in jail because my ass was guilty.

"Daddy look!" BJ yelled. Once he had my attention, he slid down the slide with McKinley right behind him. When he landed, he quickly turned around to catch her and helped her stand up. He was so naturally protective of her. They both looked up in my direction and I smiled and encouraged them.

Lauryn would be here soon after her doctor's appointment to

pick them up so that I could head over to the office and get some work done.

After Lauryn dropped by the park following her appointment and picked up the kids, I made my way over to the office. I would normally utilize my home office, but the vibe was off at home. I was greeted by the receptionist when I walked in then bombarded by Christine, my assistant.

"Mr. Smith have you had the chance to look at the contract for the Social Xchange event?"

"Nah, not yet."

"Sir, might I remind you that they want to have this event in another month and both parties will need time to plan."

"Yeah." I kept moving towards my office and knew she was following me. When I took a seat at my desk, she was standing on the other side swiping through her iPad. She sighed.

"Brandon, both Kevin and Eric have already looked it over and provided their input. We are just waiting on you to move forward. Can you find the time to prioritize this today so they can stop calling and emailing me for an update that I don't have? You're making me look bad boss." The corner of her mouth hitched up and she smile. I looked at her with disinterest, but I knew she was right. It was my fault anyway. Although we paid lawyers to look over shit like that It was my bright idea that nothing gets final approval until we all gave the greenlight and that meant combing through every page.

"Fine. I'll look it over right now. It will be in your hands before I leave today." I fished it out of the stack of documents and waved it at her.

"Any messages or updates for me?" Christine took that time to brief me on all upcoming appointments and shit that I needed to do or approve. Afterwards I dismissed her and proceeded to get through all this paperwork.

I glanced up and realized that the sun was setting. When I checked my watch, it was going on seven. I was so into my work that I'd lost track of time. My phone pinged and I had a couple of text messages I hadn't heard come through. Julissa's name caught my attention first because I didn't know when the last time she texted or called me when I was out. The message was short and straight to the point.

JuJu Bean: The baby is coming!

JuJu Bean: Where the hell are you?

JuJu Bean: She will kill you if you miss this!!!

"Shit!" That was thirty minutes ago. I jumped up and quickly grabbed my things. I slapped the contract on Christine's desk and ignored whatever she was attempting to say. I sprinted my big ass out of the office, to my truck, and made my way to Eric's.

After entering my codes to get into the gate and then the house I made my way upstairs, following the sounds of voices and music. Based on the contemporary R&B sound I knew it was one of Lauryn's playlist. Lauryn was bent over on her knees and Eric was massaging her back from behind. There was a pool in the middle of the room. Julissa was adding oils to what I now knew was a diffuser thanks to the two Zen-bougie women in my life. The room began to give off a sweet smell that even began to relax me. There were two women in the room that I didn't recognize but I guessed that they were there to assist with the labor. Julissa turned and looked at me before she went about lighting candles. I hated that we were in this weird space. Lauryn released a rush of air then sat up straight.

"Mmm. You made it. I thought I was going to have to kill my husband's only best friend." Her face held a goofy expression. She winked at me. She put on her best face, but she looked exhausted.

"Hey sis. How ya feeling?"

"Ready to get this little monster out of me." She hummed and rubbed her stomach. Eric held her arm and walked with her around the room.

"Hey, watch what you call my baby." Tears welled up in Lauryn's eyes and she snatched away from him.

"I thought that I was your baby! Bizzie." She held her hand out for me.

"Are you serious? Baby!"

I laughed and shook my head at Eric as I took his place walking

Lauryn around the room.

"Dawg she's been like this all week. I will be glad when my little princess makes her debut."

"Uhh, I can here you. I'm having a baby; I'm not fucking deaf! I swear this is the last time I let you put a baby in me." Eric looked up from his phone and narrowed his eyes in our direction.

"Gone somewhere with that schoolgirl. You still giving me my boy."

"You are not going to sit up in here and talk about her having another baby while she's trying to focus on getting this one out. Stop antagonizing her. You know chica is sensitive. Here." Julissa shoved a cup of ice chips in Eric's hand. She and one of the other women assisted Lauryn with getting into the inflatable tub.

"You are almost ready Mrs. Banks. Those contractions are coming faster, and you are almost fully dilated."

"Eric!" Lauryn's shrieked and her eyes expanded in fear. We all knew she loved being pregnant but was deathly afraid of labor. Eric tossed his shirt on the bed and climbed in behind her. He rubbed his hands up and down her arms and thighs as he spoke into her ear. No one could hear what he was saying but whatever it was Lauryn nodded, smiled and was visibly more relaxed. Eric kissed the side of her face. I looked over a Julissa who was looking at them with longing in her eyes. She busied herself with something else when she noticed me looking.

Twenty minutes later, Lauryn was screaming and cursing as she experienced one contraction after the next. The woman with the braids who looked about our age asked Eric to help her remove her bottoms. When Lauryn sat back again and opened her legs wide, I turned around to leave.

"Yoooo! Hey, that's my cue. I'll be right outside."

"No! No! Bizzie don't leave. Why would you leave me like this! I'm supposed to be your little sister." Lauryn broke down crying again. Eric gave me an apologetic look.

"Just keep your eyes above the waist Biz."

Fuck. I was trying to get my ass up out of there. I'd seen what childbirth looked like firsthand and I wasn't planning on having a front row seat to it any time soon. I nodded and took a seat facing her back. Eric grabbed the cup and fed her some ice while Julissa massaged her shoulders. My heart swelled at how nurturing and patient she was with Lauryn. She was her strength and refused to let her give up. Her voice was almost as loud as Eric's as we all urged her to keep pushing; E at her right, Ju at her left and me at her back. When she bared down and growled while she made that final push the room fell into an eerie silence. Absent was the shrill cry of a child that was just born. We all sat in place, frozen and unable to move. Lauryn leaned her head back; she was exhausted. My heart pounded in my chest. Mine and Julissa's hands found each other while we waited for her cries. *God please don't do this to them.* I didn't have the strongest relationship with God, but I was growing. I studied my Bible and went to church whenever Lauryn guilted me into it. Tonight, I felt strongly compelled to pray, so I did. I don't know how, but the words and scriptures flowed effortlessly. I prayed for a miracle. I prayed over my goddaughter and I prayed that we would survive if this didn't go in our favor. When someone mentioned calling 9-1-1, Lauryn cried Eric's name who jumped up and rushed over to where they were attending to the baby.

"What is happening? Is she okay? Say something dammit! Please!" Lauryn's voice trembled. She fought to remain calm, but it was apparent that her resolve was slowly crumbling. My fucking heart pounded so damn hard, it hurt; my hand gripped Lauryn's shoulder and the other still interlaced with Julissa's. *God please!* Then, just like that, the strongest most beautiful cry filled the space. My goddaughter announced that she was here and that she was a fighter. The room erupted in cheers of elation and tears. Lauryn's shoulders shook as she cried. I kissed her on the forehead and hugged Ju from behind. I swiped away my tears with the back of my hand. This shit had me bitching up. Eric approached us, proudly holding his youngest baby girl securely on his chest. He kneeled down next to Lauryn and planted a kiss on her lips before handing her the baby. He had that proud dad look on his face. My man was the father of another little lady that will have him wrapped around her tiny finger. I looked at Julissa who was looking upon the baby adoringly. She blushed this time when she caught me looking.

"Thank you, baby. Once again you did an amazing job Mrs. Banks. Family, meet Noelle Starr Banks."

JULISSA

After making sure that Lauryn and Eric were settled in for the night, I'd finally made it home. Home... This place hadn't felt like home for some time now. Brandon hadn't been feeling me lately since the whole Ethan debacle. He had me on ice which was extremely difficult for me because everything about this man turned me on. Every morning I watched him saunter into the bathroom, his boxer briefs low on is waist and his solid, thick build turned me on. I relished in the fact that he was so much bigger than me and that beast between his legs made my stomach flutter. I shook away the images that had me forming a wet spot in my panties. I was addicted to him and I was overdue for a hit. Brandon had a very healthy sexual appetite. He couldn't get enough. Most days I couldn't help but wonder if he was giving it to someone else, more specifically Jaynah, but I didn't have the courage to ask. It was important for me not to give him another reason to be mad at me. Aside from the physical I missed talking to him. I missed his friendship.

"Ugh!" I grunted in frustration. Time for another cold shower. Matter of fact, why was I still here? I couldn't answer the questioned that I'd been asking myself for the last week. Well, that was a lie. This man had me rewired to fit his specifications and to only work for him. I could never give myself to another man after rekindling our love. As I got closer to the bedroom I was led by the smell of tobacco and vanilla. The room glowed from the candlelight. Brandon was on the attached balcony smoking a cigar. His eyes landed on me when I opened the double French doors. Hesitantly, I stood with my back against the doors. He motioned for me to join him and I eagerly sat next to him. He handed me the cigar and I took a couple of puffs before handing it back over to him. I took a slow sip of the glass of whiskey on the table in front of us. We sat in silence for I don't know how long, looking out into the night sky. I studied him and he kept clinching his hands. He was fighting the urge to touch me. If he only knew how bad I needed him too, but I would wait for him to decide to let me in. I'd apologized and tried to do everything I could to make it right; the ball was in his court.

"Hey. Come here."

I quickly straddled him and placed my hand on his shoulders. We both laughed. When his hands landed on my waist, I relaxed into him.

"What you did was deceptive and sneaking as hell Ju. You were sneaking around with another man behind my back. That shit was fucked up. One thing about me is that I don't share. You should know that if you have to sneak around behind my back then you're knowingly doing something that I wouldn't approve of. Do you still have feelings for him?"

"N- no..." My eyes shot down to my hands.

"I need your honesty Ju. Don't say shit because you think that's what I want to hear or because it will upset me."

"I don't have feelings for him. Do I think that he is attractive? Yes, but that is it. We had a lot in common so I thought that we could be friends. What I did was wrong. I will never do anything like that again. Brandon I will never lie to you."

"All is forgiven. I love you." My heart swelled at hearing those words and knowing that he meant it.

"I love you too."

We both leaned in and our lips met in a passionate kiss. Brandon sucked the air out of me and gave it back as his tongue darted in my mouth. He explored my mouth and tasted all of me. Brandon's kisses always left my head spinning. My pussy throbbed with need for him; it had been too long. I gripped his shirt and pulled it over his head. I took a minute to appreciate his body and traced my fingers around his upper half. He unbuckled and zipped down his pants as I lifted my maxi dress up to my waist. His mouth found my neck and he used his tongue to drive me crazy. When he sucked on my spot, I was ready.

"Brandon, please," I begged. I ground my pelvis into his rock-solid erection. He reached under my dress and tugged hard, ripping my panties. I yelped and he snickered, revealing his delicious dimple. Without preamble, he lifted me over him and eased me down onto him. I tossed my head back, looking up at the sky. There was a gentle tug at my hair and it all came cascading down from my messy bun as I rode Brandon with wild abandon. I leaned forward which allow friction between his stomach and my clit. I was already unraveling.

"Brandon," I whimpered.

"Shit Ju. That's right baby, you can let it go."

Everything in me quickly uncoiled and I bucked against him. I screamed out as my release hit me like a tsunami. I was drowning, then I was floating, then drowning again. I gasped for air while I rode the wave. Brandon's grip on me tightened and his breaths were coming out in harsh spurts. His movements were no longer deliberate and smooth. He pumped into me hard and fast and I came again, but this time he was right behind me.

"Argh. Dammit Ju. Shit!"

I rested my head over his shoulder, and he wrapped his strong arms around me as we both caught our breath. I sniffled and swiped my eyes.

"Ju are you crying?"

"No. Yes. I thought you were going to leave me." I sat up and wiped my eyes. He grinned and shook his head. When we first met, he rarely smiled. I was blessed to see it daily, but it was missing for the last week or so. I felt privileged to be able to pull them out of him.

"Nah. Don't ever worry about that, you got me."

"And you got me."

JULISSA

"**J**ulissa! Come on man. We still gotta scoop up little man! JULISSA!"

"I'm coming! DANG! Always rushing me," I mumbled to myself as I fluffed my hair and applied my favorite lip gloss. I loved it because it made my lips look even fuller; kissable. I snatched up my purse and stomped downstairs. The sight before me caused me to stumble. Brandon's wardrobe only consisted of his basic uniform; blue or black jeans, and white, black, and gray shirts, but dammit if he didn't look good enough to eat looking at me with a scowl etched in his face. He was wearing jeans and a white tee. He reached for me and held on until I was secure on my feet.

"Bring your sexy ass here."

"Brandon don't…" I attempted to push him away, but his lips made contact with mine, taking my breath away along with my lip gloss. My heart rate picked up and I squeezed my legs tight. For a split second I forgot where I was and what we were planning to do today. Knowing that look in my eyes, Brandon growled as he scooped me up. That snapped me out of my trance. I squealed and kicked my feet.

"Brandon! Back down the stairs please." We both smiled at each other. He looked at me as if I was the only thing he wanted in that moment. His need for me was palpable. I loved it. My belly fluttered.

"As soon as we get back BJ is going straight to bed," he muttered in my ear before he nipped my earlobe.

"You won't let me take my time to get ready, but you'll risk being late for some ass?"

"Hell yeah. I'm a man Julissa."

"Boy let's go."

When we pulled up to Jaynah's to pick up BJ, Brandon unlocked the door and looked over at me. I turned and gave him a look that said *what the fuck.* He exhaled out his nose and nodded towards the door.

"Julissa go get BJ."

"What? You're joking right? I know she's been cordial, but your baby momma doesn't like me. You go get him and stop playing."

"Jay needs to get used to seeing you. There may be times when I might need you to come over here and get him. I need to make sure that you two can coexist and behave when I'm not around."

"Oh, you don't have to worry about me behaving." I shot back.

"Bullshit Ju. You love taking shots and throwing shade at people you don't like. You and your petty bestie."

"Is that so? Wait until I tell Lauryn..."

"Here you go. Go get my son Julissa."

"Fine." I made sure to slam his precious car door just in case he didn't know that I was aggravated.

"Keep on fucking with me Ju!"

Pressing the doorbell, I put on my best face; a smile and all. All of that faded when the door flung open.

"What the hell are *you* doing here? Where is Bizzie?" She turned her face up at me like I was yesterday's trash then tried to look around me. I wanted to knock that stank ass look off her face.

"He's in the car waiting and where are your clothes?" Jaynah shifted her wight to her other leg to accommodate BJ's weight. She was wearing a nude lace bra and matching panties. She was also wearing a robe but left it wide open. She had a nice body and I could instantly see why he'd been attracted to her; made me wonder what he saw in me.

"First of all, this is my house. I wear whatever I want."

"And you just so happen to be wearing your thirsty gear when Brandon is scheduled to pick up BJ?"

"You know what? Where is he? I don't want my son going anywhere with you." This girl was giving me a headache. I pinched the bridge of my nose to tame my temper. After a couple of deep breaths, I was able to address her like an adult.

"Look Jaynah, if you do that Brandon is going to assume that one or the both of us can't handle this arrangement. I love Brandon and your son and I'm not going anywhere. Brandon has already asked but I am going to also ask that you not disrespect my relationship with the father of your child. You purposely wearing skimpy outfits to get his attention is going to do just that. He's a man so he may look. He may even find himself aroused, but he's going to come home every time and work that out with me. Brandon's not going anywhere. Now, I can go tell Brandon that you are refusing to let his son go and let him deal with you or you can honor your word and hand him over. He's safe with me."

We stared at each other waiting to see who would break first. It wasn't going to be me. I wasn't going to the car without BJ. We both knew Brandon was a little touched; crazy. She rolled her eyes and handed me his bag before she kissed him and placed him on the ground. I squatted down and allowed him to hug me.

"Hey little man! You ready to go?"

"Yeah!"

"Okay, well tell mommy bye."

"Bye, bye mama." He blew his momma a kiss. We walked hand in hand to the truck. Brandon got out to help with getting him into his car seat. I ignored him and got back into the car.

"What the hell took you so long?"

"Not right now Brandon."

"So you got an attitude now? If we…"

"Not right now. We can discuss this when BJ is not listening." I gritted my teeth. Brandon snatched BJ's bag from my hand and my arm cocked back on instinct. His eyes darkened and narrowed.

"Ju I wish you would." He pulled out headphones and a tablet and handed them BJ, who knew exactly what to do."

"You the one snatching shit from me."

"Yo, my bad, but what happened?"

"Are you sleeping with her?"

"WHAT? No!" I leaned forward and stared into his eyes. He had the audacity to laugh and push me back.

"Yo, Get out of my face man. What is this really about?"

"Does Jaynah always greet you half naked when you pick him up?"

"Yeah, but she wants me so what do you expect?" He shrugged his shoulder. I couldn't believe what I was hearing.

"You are so damn arrogant. That's not appropriate Biz. It's disrespectful and it's fucked up."

"Which is why I sent you to the door. Maybe next time she'll think twice before she plans to seduce me."

"Oh, her ass will definitely think twice. Just give me a heads-up next time. I almost blacked out on that girl."

"My bad Ju." We rode the remainder of the way in silence. I texted Lauryn letting her know that we were on the way for dinner and briefly explained the stunt that Jaynah tried to pull.

"Baby?"

"Yeah?"

"What was she wearing?" My mouth dropped before my face hardened. Brandon tossed his head back and laughed. Seeing him on the verge of tears pulled a laugh out of me. He uncrossed my arms and kissed my hand.

"I can't stand you sometimes."

"But you love me though."

Lauryn and Eric greeted us at the door. She was wearing a coral maxi dress and her feet were bare. Noelle was nestled securely in her arms. McKinley was sitting on Eric's shoulder's but demanded to be put down as soon as her eyes landed on BJ. I held my arms out for Noelle and Lauryn gently placed her in my arms.

"I cannot believe that you have two children."

"We can't either. Sometimes I just watch them sleep, appreciating every breath that their little bodies take. I don't know what I've done to receive these two blessings."

"Yeah, you should hear what she says when they're wide-awake driving us insane like today," Eric added. We all laughed and made our way inside.

"Don't act like they don't drive you nuts some days."

"Facts."

"I'm going to take them upstairs to my mom. She came over to help out for a little bit. Ju you want to come with me?"

"Sure. I haven't seen your mom in a while."

After we got the kids settled we made our way back downstairs to have dinner and catch up with each other. Brandon and Eric were in front of the TV watching ESPN. I still didn't understand their obsession with watching a game then watching footage and other men talk about a game they already saw.

"Okay you two. Let's eat before my mom has to go!"

"Ain't gotta tell me twice," Eric mumbled then slapped her on the butt.

The meal was catered and consisted of steak, lobster, mashed potatoes and asparagus. For dessert we had adult milk shakes. I was stuffed.

"Dinner was amazing guys!"

"It would have been better if my husband would allow me to cook. I haven't had to lift a finger since I had Noelle, unless it pertains to her and her sister."

"Seriously? I would love to have someone wait on me hand and foot, especially make all my meals, drinks, and snacks? Shoot. Sounds like you're living the life to me."

"Spoiled ass," Brandon mumbled and Eric held his drink up in agreement."

"Hey! Sunday dinner is our tradition and it's important that we participate in cooking the meal. Cooking and baking makes me feel good. I just feel useless now." Lauryn pouted and was almost on the verge of tears. I gave the men at the table a warning to stop picking on her. Her emotions had been all over the place and she was still fighting through postpartum depression.

"Don't do that Lauryn. Eric loves you and he just wants to make this transition to two kiddos as seamless as possible for you.

I'll come back over later this week and we can bake a bunch of sweets."

"I'd like that. Thank you." My bestie was spoiled, but she'd earned it. She was always putting others before herself; she deserved to be treated. I don't know what I would have done without her friendship. I could call her at any time of the day, and she was there, no matter what. It was Lauryn who got me through some major break ups including the one with Brandon. I looked over at her and there was that signature spark in her eyes again.

"How are things with you two? I'm so glad you guys worked things out. You did work things out, right?"

"Yeah sis we did. I love my JuJu bean."

I choked on my shake. It felt like I was hacking up a lung. Brandon patted my back, hard, which only made it worst. I was trying to tell him to stop and couldn't get it out.

"Brandon you're killing her. Stop!" Lauryn hollered.

I reached for my cup and took a sip of my water. "I can't believe you called me that in front of them."

"What?" He flashed an innocent smile and kissed me on the top of my forehead. "Lauryn don't start."

"Aww... you love her... Y'all are so cute." Brandon got up from the table.

"E, I got some business that I need to discuss with you." He patted his pocket and Eric eased up from the table.

"Follow me."

"Take that outside! Do not smoke in this house you two!" Lauryn waited until she heard the back door open and close.

"Come on. Let's clean up, check on my babies and make us some big girl drinks. I need all the details!"

BIZZIE

We sat back lounging in Eric's backyard. I handed Eric a joint and lit one of my own.

"You need to try this shit. Saint put me on. You know this nigga makes his own shit? I'm trying to convince him to go the legal route and open up a few shops in Colorado and Vegas. Get into CBD oil, shit like that, but you know that nigga love the streets."

"Just like how we did. Saint is still young. He's addicted to that fast life." Eric pulled from his joint, looked at it and mouthed the word *damn*. "This is some good shit. Damn."

"What I tell you? And he can tell you everything about the makings of this shit. He's like some hood botanist."

"Botanist? What you know about that?"

"Bruh, I read. I don't need no college degree to know shit." I glared at Eric. I knew he was just joking but he wasn't about to just question my intelligence like that.

"Nah, I know that. Who would have thought all those years ago I would be hanging out in my backyard of my own home talking with my best friend about botany?"

"We still smoking weed though and this shit is a damn estate, E. You sure you only planning on having one more kid?" I waved my hand around to demonstrate the expanse of his property. He leaned back and sighed.

"No. Well, *I* want more but I'm working hard to convince wifey to try one more time for a boy, so I know I ain't getting a fourth. As long as we try one more time, I'll be cool."

"Shit, mess around and have five girls running you crazy."

"Man, don't even speak that. I think God is teaching me a lesson from how I use to treat women."

"Maybe." The corners of my mouth turned up involuntarily. I was high as shit but felt like I could still function. It didn't leave me stuck. Eric leaned forward on his knees and trained his eyes on me.

"You and Ju really straight?" I leaned back and ran my hand down my face.

"Yeah. We're figuring things out. She drives me crazy sometimes. One minute she's this mature ambitious woman who's about her business and knows what she wants. The next she's this impulsive, flaky, crazy ass person I barely recognize, but I guess all that's her. You know she was in the shower one night and I found myself checking her phone." Eric laughed mid-inhale and choked.

"Nigga you what?" He coughed, trying to clear his throat.

"Exactly. I went through her phone like a bitch. You know me! I ain't never felt the need to do no shit like that. I've never given a damn. Julissa got my head fucked up."

"That's love. I think love is the closest thing to insanity. Being in love is like riding a crazy ass rollercoaster and when you think things are calming down that shit starts back up again."

"Yo! I find myself reading certain shit just so she doesn't have to go to another nigga to talk about it. Got me reading poetry and shit. Like nah baby, we gonna talk about this. That type of shit had her hanging out with that poet. He won't be a problem anymore though."

"Yo B, I hope you ain't go and do nothing stupid."

"Nah, I just bought the B-Side." Eric busted out laughing and we bumped fists.

"Yeah, your ass is wide open."

"I won't even try to lie. I love that woman to death. Be honest with me, if you could do it all over again with Lauryn, would you have pursued her?"

"In a heartbeat. That shit wasn't even a well thought out

choice. I was drawn to her. She literally pulled me into her universe, and it was a world of unexplainable peace and calm. She provided stability that I didn't even know I needed. Lauryn helped me to see that there was a life, a good life waiting for me if I left the streets."

Eric didn't even blink before he responded. My dude had his heart captured by a good girl and she was exactly what he needed. We were some wild ass boys. I was starting to understand what he felt when he first met her, and I tried to get him to leave her alone. I didn't know if Julissa and I would have a love like our friends, but we would define it for ourselves and create our own special story. Eric looked down at his watch.

"It's my babies' bedtime. I promised Kin that I would read to her tonight. She'll be even more excited that her uncle Bizzie is going to help."

"Bruh, you lucky I love that little girl. BJ don't get no stories unless it's from Julissa. His ass probably all up under her knocked out already." I stood up and stretched out my limbs before I followed him into the house. I still couldn't believe that this was our new normal, but I was rocking with it.

"Tonight was fun and much needed. I'm glad we got to help them have some grown up time. They seem to have adjusted well. Lauryn is still struggling to feel herself again, but counseling has helped her so much. You need to talk to your friend and tell him to stop bringing up having more babies. He's stressing her out."

Julissa was rambling. It's what she did when she was excited and didn't know what to do with all of that energy, but I had a few ideas of where she could transfer that too. She was in the middle of slipping off her shoes, but I pulled her up and attacked her mouth. Immediately she started to climb up my body. I loved that she was always ready. I held her up by her ass and massaged each cheek while our tongues intertwined and danced around each other.

"Daaaaad! Aaaaah a monster!" I groaned and Julissa giggled. She climbed down and headed for the bathroom. Her curvy hips swayed to a beat that I couldn't hear, but I felt that shit.

"I'll start the shower and you go take care of the monsters."

I jogged to BJ's room. His nightlight illuminated his dinosaur themed room, so I didn't bother turning on the room light. The covers where pulled over his head. I sat in the chair next to the bed and gently pulled the covers down.

"Little man, what's up?

"There's a monster over there." He whimpered and pointed at nothing in particular.

"Remember what daddy told you about monsters?"

"Yes." One tear slipped down his face and I scooped him up and placed him on my lap.

"Who's the biggest monster of them all?" A sly smile formed on my face and his lit up.

"You are."

"That's right! Ain't no monster brave enough to come in here and mess with *my* son. You just tell them that your daddy's home and watch them disappear. The secret is that you have to believe it when you say it. Got it?"

"Okay," he whimpered again.

"Come on man, you can do better than that."

"Yes!" This time, he said it with as much conviction as a three-year-old could muster.

"So, what do you tell those monsters?"

"MY DADDY IS HERE, SO GET THE FUCK OUT!" he yelled at the top of his lungs.

"Woah! Okay. Very good, but you can't say fuck. That's a bad word. Okay?"

"Okay daddy." I rustled the hair on the top of his head where I planted a kiss.

"Aight, now let's get you back in bed." BJ crawled out of my lap and back into his bed. I tucked him in and sat with him until he finally nodded off.

Thankfully Julissa took long ass showers. She was under the water rinsing her hair while she sang some song in Spanish. When I stepped in behind her, I wrapped my arms around her and caressed her stomach with my thumbs. My moves matched the swaying of her hips. My tongue traced around her outer ear. I smiled when she squirmed and laid her head back onto my chest.

"You want a baby?" I whispered in her ear.

Julissa quickly spun around and studied my face. Her eyelids fluttered as she blinked away the dripping water.

"What did Eric have you over there smoking?" Her hands roamed all over my body and I hummed my approval.

"Nothing. Well, we were smoking but… You're so good with BJ and the girls. You never talk about whether or not you want kids."

"Kids? As in more than one?"

"Stop stalling." The muscles in my jaw twitched.

"Why can't we talk about this later? I was hoping that we could…"

Julissa's words faded away as she squatted down and her warm, wet mouth took me in. I knew she was stalling but my current position left me at her mercy. My hands found her head and I grasped a handful of her hair. This woman could do unspeakable things with her mouth. My baby was nasty. A guttural moan escaped my lips as I released my seed in record time. She licked me clean and allowed the water to rinse away the rest. She stood up with a smug look of satisfaction written all over her beautiful face. She got off on making me her bitch.

"Got dammit baby. You about to get my damn gangsta card pulled." I smacked her ass then pulled her to the bed where I crawled in between her legs and returned the favor until she begged for mercy.

My eyes felt heavy as I lazily ran my hands through Julissa's soft curls. We went at it for another three rounds before we showered again and changed the sheets. The latest action flick was playing on the TV, but my mind was elsewhere. It was like I was obsessed with the thought of having a family with Julissa.

"So, you don't want kids?" Julissa laughed and sat up.

"You're not going to let this go, are you?"

"I mean I'm just saying. You might already be pregnant so we might as well talk about it."

"Mr. Smith, are you *trying* to get me pregnant?" I licked my lips and flashed a look that told her that I was dead ass serious. Truth be told, I couldn't tell you where this was coming from, so I understood her confusion. Julissa rolled her eyes and blew out a rush of air.

"Yes Brandon, I want kids. I've always wanted kids. I just want it to be at the right time. I want to be established in my career where I can put someone else in charge and focus on being an awesome mom. I'm not even on the best terms with my family right now. I have a lot of stuff to get in order."

"Do you want kids with me?" I avoided her eyes.

"Brandon... Of course, I do. You're a great dad and you're so good with McKinley and Noelle. Why would you even think otherwise?"

I shrugged my shoulder and tried not to fall back into thinking that no one would seriously want a family with me. My own family didn't want me so... yeah. She sat up and held my face in her hands. Her bright brown eyes bored into me.

"Do you want to talk about it?" Julissa knew that I didn't have any family other than them. She just didn't know about all the disturbing shit I went through when I was with my biological family. Memories of that shit use to give me nightmares, but I hadn't had one since she and I got back together. I sniffed and shook my head.

"Nah, I'm good. With BJ, he was... I love my son, but he wasn't planned. Fatherhood never crossed my mind. Jay and I wasn't together. We just use to kick it every now and then. This is the first time that I ever thought about it in this way, I guess. Just wanted to see where your head was at."

"You want to be my baby daddy? You want to be my baby daddy." She bounced on the bed and sang. Her infectious smile lit up the room. I couldn't help the laugh that escaped my mouth.

"Yo, calm your ass down. You're being real corny right now. How about we take a little trip; just me and you. No nutty ass friends, no work, no kids, no baby mamas, just the two of us out somewhere doing grown folks' shit."

"Hell yeah! This is exciting! Where we going? I think..."

"Don't think. I'll handle everything. You just get everything squared away with work and pack a bag."

JULISSA

We woke up early Friday morning and made our way to the airport. Brandon still hadn't told me where we were going. He simply instructed me to pack for both hot and cool weather. The entire way to the airport I worked on getting him to reveal our destination because the suspense of it all was killing me. He simply kept on his poker face and ignored me as long as I asked about details of our trip. After we were all checked in, we found a spot to eat breakfast. I was still struggling to wake up since my excitement wouldn't allow me to sleep, so I ordered a cortadito, which was pretty much expresso, steamed milk and sugar. While I sipped on my drink, Brandon slid his phone across the table. It was our digital boarding passes.

"Vegas? Are you crazy?" I squealed and woke up the entire restaurant. "Yay! I am sooo excited." I clapped my hands and shimmied in my seat. Brandon looked at me adoringly and flashed a boyish grin.

"I still can't believe that you've traveled all over the world, but never been to Vegas. This use to be me and Eric's spot when we first started making money."

"It just wasn't at the top of my list, but I am ecstatic to be going with you. I needed a change of atmosphere. Do you gamble?"

"I play a little blackjack."

"Not a slot machine type of guy?"

"Not at all. I don't fuck with them shits. I'll teach you."

"You sure?" He nodded. "Okay, I will hold you too that."

When Brandon first mentioned that we were going to Vegas I was a little skeptical, but now that we made it, I was starting to think that this man knew me better than I knew myself. It was the perfect place to relax and turn up. There was so much to do and so many lights; my senses were in overload. We had a suite at the Mandalay Bay with all the amenities. I felt like a celebrity. When we entered the suite, my mouth fell open. There were candles strategically placed all over the room, creating a sensual glow. Dark purple flower petals were sprinkled around multiple gift boxes on the bed.

"Brandon. Aww babe," I cooed. He tilted his head down to hide his bashful smile. I took my time taking everything in. On the table sat a bottle of my favorite champagne and an assortment of chocolate covered fruit. I felt myself getting emotional and laughed it off. He did all of this for me. My body began to heat with not just desire for this puzzle of a man, but love. No other man had ever made me feel so cared for and appreciated. When I turned around to express my gratitude Brandon was already on me. He kissed me with so much hunger and need that he had my head spinning. Then his mouth and hands were everywhere as I struggled to keep up. I literally ached for him. He chuckled in my ear before he backed up and pulled me towards the bed; he knew exactly what he was doing to me. Brandon was slowly disarming me and letting me know that he was in control tonight and I wasn't going to fight him. I wholly trusted him with the task of bringing my body to its peak over and over. We spent the remainder of the morning and afternoon in bed sexing and worshipping each other's body before sleep took us both down.

When we finally came up for air, we ordered room service since Brandon was adamant about fruit and chocolate not being a real meal. After lunch, we sat on the balcony where he taught me how to play blackjack. He was so patient with me even when I could tell he wanted to say something slick shit about me being slow to catch on, but once I caught it, I had it. That evening we dressed up and hit the casino. I wore the dress, shoes, and jewelry that Brandon surprised me with inside of those beautifully wrapped gift boxes. Surprisingly, he had a good eye because the clothes weren't what I would have picked out for myself but looked and fit amazing on me. I joked about him switching careers to a fashion stylist, but he wasn't having that. We looked good together dressed to the nines; bad ass. We walked around for a bit hand-in-hand then made a beeline straight for the blackjack table. I thought that we would play together but Brandon pulled up a chair for me to take a shot at it.

An hour later, I was five thousand dollars richer and walked around with a lopsided grin on my face. Brandon made reservations at a popular restaurant for dinner and we were going to hit up a club after that. He bumped my shoulder.

"You did well grasshopper." His deep gritty voice mumbled.

"What can I say? I had a great teacher. Hey, did you plan anything outside of Vegas?"

"Nah." He turned his mouth down and shook his head. I perked up even more.

"Can I suggest something for tomorrow morning?" Brandon eyed me suspiciously but relented.

"Alright. What do you want to do?"

We woke up early the next morning, hired a car service and made our way to Arizona to see the Grand Canyon. We were supposed to rent a car and drive, but Brandon took me to the strip club after dinner, and we had a little too much fun between the partying, the shots and edibles. He was surprised that I was so comfortable there. Truth be told, it wasn't my first time at a strip club, but I wasn't going to tell him that. When one of the dancers pulled me up on the private stage to work the pole, Brandon looked on in awe at how I performed a few tricks thanks to the pole dancing classes Lauryn and I secretly took. I never felt sexier or more alive. He was speechless when I paid for us to get a couple's lap dance. The dancer was young and cute. She had a sweet and sultry disposition. She respected that we were a couple and did her best to engage the both of us. Brandon thought that she actually liked me more than him. That shit only turned the both of us on and we ended up screwing each other in the private room, then again when we got back to our room.

Now, here we were paying for our sinful night, hungover, hell, still drunk, donning shades and sipping Pedialyte out of water bottles. I'd gotten up early and found a convenience store to load up on snacks, water, and sandwiches to allow Brandon to sleep in. He was grumpy in the mornings, but I knew when we got to our destination his disposition would brighten up. The drive would sober us up. I rested my head on his shoulder and enjoyed the scenery. The desert was beautiful in its own special way and the sunrises here were heavenly. It felt like we were in another world. When Brandon's large hand clasped my thigh, I smiled and snuggled up closer.

"Can I talk now?" I giggled and he chuckled.

"Am I that bad in the morning?" He turned to face me; his forehead wrinkled.

"Only when you don't get all of your sleep. Actually, you're *not* a morning person at all."

"Is that why you be so quiet in the mornings now?"

"Duh. You don't remember that time I jumped in the bed with you and did my good morning dance? You literally gave me the death stare and told me to shut up and go find some business." He broke out in a full-blown laugh and wrapped his arm around me. I poked my bottom lip out and he leaned in and sucked on it. I was now wet with desire for him, but the most spectacular views came into site, cooled me down and shifted my focus.

"Look! Oh my God, we're here!" The interstate led us right along the canyon, giving us a perfect view.

"There are places we can pull over if you all would like," the driver spoke.

I bit my bottom lip and looked up at Brandon. He kissed me and nodded.

"Yes please." As soon as the car stopped, I was pushing Brandon out of the SUV.

As I looked out into the Grand Canyon, a gasp escaped from my open mouth. I felt Brandon's warmth and he embraced me from behind.

"This is just amazing. So beautiful. I can't believe that we are here."

"Yeah, it is pretty amazing isn't it? Is this it?"

"No, silly. There's an actual park. Let's see if we could do a tour."

Now when I said do a tour, I have to admit that I did not think it all the way through. I didn't think it would be hiking and somewhat risky. I took a step back as the tour guide explained our route and precautions. Brandon noticed that I was hesitant and pulled me back.

"Ain't no way I'm letting you chicken out on your own excursion. Baby you got this." The park ranger began his trek and the group followed.

"But what if I fall and sprain my ankle? You know that I'm clumsy."

"Would I ever let you fall?"

"You better not! Ah shit." My foot clipped a rock and I stumbled. Brandon caught me and stopped my fall.

"Julissa."

"No. You wouldn't let me fall." I sighed and wiped the sweat off of my brow. The tour was great. We learned about the formation of the Grand Canyon and the history of the area. I think Brandon enjoyed the tour more than I did. If I even attempted to make a comment, he'd flash me a look of exasperation because he was so into what the tour guide was saying. I spent most of it trying not to trip and fall to my untimely death. By the time we made it back to our ride, the sun was beginning to set. I got our driver to take a few pictures of us to capture the magical moment. I stood on my toes and kissed Brandon passionately. His large hands gripped my ass and I blushed.

"This was fun today. Thanks for trusting me." He nibbled on my neck and I giggled.

"Do you trust me Ju?"

"With everything in me." I gazed into his eyes and tugged at his beard.

"Come on, I got an idea. No questions though."

I regarded him suspiciously but agreed.

"Okay."

• •

"Friend you are glowing! Did you enjoy the trip?"

"Lauryn it was amazing. I was gifted to see another side of Brandon. He is such a good man; so many layers."

"Yeah, yeah, yeah. But what about the sex? I know he blew that back out!" Monica stuck her tongue out and danced in her seat. We were having brunch at one of our favorite spots on the beach. It was Lauryn's first day away from the kids since she had baby Noelle. I stuck my tongue out at Monica and rolled my eyes.

"Nah buddy. This one is a keeper. I'm not kissing and telling. Anyway, he was relaxed and open to doing whatever." My mind traveled back to what would forever be cherished memories. Lauryn slapped the table.

"You are so in love with him!"

"I am. I've never denied that."

"No. I mean like that *forever, let's go half on a baby* type of love. It's all over you. No one is more deserving of this than you. I am happy for you JuJu bean." We all laughed at her using Brandon's nickname for me.

"Bitch if you ever in your life call me that again. Brandon makes me happy, but enough of all the mushy stuff chicas. Thank you, Lauryn, for helping Draya with the covers. You already know that's not really my thing, so I was thinking that you can come on as a contracted designer and I can have a specific division for books."

"Ju, you know my hands are full," Lauryn whined.

"Girl what is the problem?" Monica questioned with sass. Lauryn glared at her and ran her hand down her natural tapered cut. They had a minor fall out when she and Eric were going through their shit. She kept a tight circle during that time and left Monica out a lot. Because of that, I never knew if they would get along or not when we linked up.

"The problem is that I have a newborn and a two-year-old and a grown ass baby husband. I'm tired."

"Please Lauryn. I promise I won't take on any client without pulling you into the consultations and I will only do one or two projects a month. Think it over. I'll get you that new stroller/car seat combo you wanted."

"Oh sis Eric already caved in and got it for me." She waved me off. "I'll think about it though."

"That's all I'm asking. Thank you!"

"So, what did you bring us back from Vegas?" She smiled and tried to peek inside the bags that were next to me.

"Brandon's right. You are spoiled as hell bestie."

BIZZIE

This day couldn't end soon enough. I was tired and drained. I spent most of the last two days putting out fires. It was time to put some new people on my team because a couple of employees I put in charge were fucking up royally. There was the manager at one of my spots that ordered a shit load of the wrong liquor and another had a sexual harassment charge filed against him by a female employee. The girl was a young college student and he was about ten years older than her. The look on his face when I brought up the complaint told me everything I needed to know so I fired him on the spot. Now, I needed to find a replacement because I never wanted to overextend my staff.

I sat at my desk checking the books. My accounting was something I never trusted anyone with one hundred percent and that's coming from someone with a supreme finance team; the best of the best.

"Fuck." I cursed when the numbers weren't adding up for me. My mood was shitty, so I chose to work later than normal. One thing about me was that I always tried my best not to direct my horrible moods on to other people, especially my son and my lady. Julissa and I had been going strong since we returned from Vegas. She'd moved in and changed up my whole spot with the exception of my office, gym, and BJ's room. We were polar opposites but were managing well. She and I both understood the importance of giving each other space when needed. She allowed me to be myself and I loved her for that. Truth be told, it only made me want to be better for her. It bothered me that she was still at odds with her family, but I didn't want to push the issue. It would only make her stubborn ass push back more. I'd give her a little more time before I called her out. Julissa was the true definition of ride or die and I don't know what I did to deserve her.

"Screw this." I shut everything down and decided to finally make my way home. I was missing my lady and in need of her cooking.

When the front door shut behind me, I secured the lock. The house was dimly lit and hip-hop music was playing, but the volume was low.

"Hey! Ju!" I made my way to the family room which was her favorite spot in the house. There she was. Standing in the middle of the room, curls wild and all over her head, a bashful smile. She was wearing cotton shorts that hit just below her cheeks and a black tank, her feet were bare. Julissa held a round cake with a candle burning.

"Happy Birthday baby."

No matter how simple this was, her gesture had me choking up. I opened my mouth to speak but the words eluded me. When she started singing happy birthday, my eyes watered and I sniffed, then blinked them back. The emotions that flooded over me were overwhelming, but she kept singing and like gravity, I moved towards her almost involuntarily. She held the cake up to me. I raised my eyebrow and tilted my head back.

"Brandon! Make a wish and blow." The light of the flames illuminated her perfect face. I nodded and closed my eyes like I'd seen other people do and made my first birthday wish before blowing out the candle. Julissa whistled and cheered before placing the cake on the bar top.

"I've never had that before."

"Hmm? Never had what?"

"This. The birthday cake, the song, you know."

"No one has every sang happy birthday to you or given you a cake?"

"Nah, I didn't grow up celebrating birthdays and E and I would just tell each other happy birthday and get fucked up." I removed my shirt and my belt while I walked up on her. She was pinned between me and the bar. My lips pressed against her soft supple ones and I eased my tongue in. She tasted like Moscato.

"Thank you." I slowly licked up her neck. "I love you." My fingers trailed up her thighs, then tugged at the waistband of her shorts. On instinct she lifted each leg until she was relieved of her shorts. She wasn't wearing underwear and I growled before ripping off her shirt and sitting her on top of the bar. She leaned back on her elbows and her lust filled eyes darkened as she watched me kick of my shoes then removed my bottoms. Julissa smirked with her luscious bottom lip tucked between her teeth. Falling to my knees, I hooked her legs on my arms and immediately attacked her clit. I needed her to get hers first but fast; she already had me about to explode. I teased and tortured her, writing my name on her with my tongue. She was marked as mine. When her legs began to shake and she began to grind against my face, I stood up and slowly slipped into her as she came undone.

"Ah, ah, ah! Ooooo Brandon. Sssshit!" She wrapped her arms around my neck and met me thrust for thrust. We may have been polar opposites, but we were equals in the bedroom. Our hands frantically grasped at each other's sweat slicked skin. Julissa's hand wandered down my back and over my ass. I tensed.

"Ju..."

"I love you baby." She purred then licked up my Adam's apple, then kissed under my chin. I felt the invasion and pressure between my asshole and nuts but before I could react an indescribable pleasure washed over me. I tossed my head back and rammed into her like a teen getting his first piece of ass. My grown ass howled.

"Fuuuuck... Got dammit Ju!" She was paying me no mind because she was in the middle of her own orgasm. Julissa's legs tightened around me and she cried out. Evidence of her release ran down our bodies. I held on to her and brought her down to the floor with me. Our heavy breathing filled the room.

"Don't ever do that shit again Ju."

"Why not? You should have seen your reaction. Like your eyes rolled back and your mouth fell open as you surrendered to the pleasure. Hmm. It was amazing!" She kissed my chest then rested her head and drew lazy circles around my ribs.

"Whatever." I mumbled. I didn't know what I was going to do with the girl. I tried to fight the sleep that was claiming me. Julissa lifted up off of me. A warm rag landing on my stomach jolted me out of my sleep.

"Clean up and come get some cake."

I stood up and wiped off. "You already gave me that."

By the time I slipped on my boxers and got comfortable on the couch she had already cut one big slice for us to share.

"Is that Lauryn's red velvet cake?"

"It is. Made especially for you." She sat next to me and stretched her legs across my lap. I opened my mouth to receive the first piece of cake. This was a birthday I would never forget. We talked and caught up on our day while we fed each other cake. The shit was good as hell. Life was good as hell.

JULISSA

"Where did I put my other shoe?" I was in the closet looking for my other blue ballet flat. I was running late and was supposed to be at the office thirty minutes ago.

"Seriously baby?" Brandon was looking down at me holding the heel that I'd just tossed away. "You almost took my head off with this. What are you doing?"

"I'm looking for my other blue shoe." I plopped down on the floor and whined.

"You mean this?" He smirked and handed me my other shoe. "It was under the bed."

"Thank you! I am so late." I slipped on my shoes and dashed out of the closet. Brandon caught me by the waist and pushed his pelvis up against me. My cha cha throbbed in response, but I had absolutely no time to do anything about it.

"Slow your roll. Remember you're picking up BJ from school today since I have that late business meeting."

"Yep. I'm going to take him to the park, then back home for dinner and dessert. We are going to make some sugar cookies. Just make sure that you are home in time for dinner Brandon."

"Ju I can't make any promises."

"I don't want your promises I want your commitment!" I shoved my way out of his arms. Lately, I'd been having dinner alone or after nine in the evening when I did wait for him. I was also helping more with BJ which I didn't mind, but this wasn't like him not to make time for us.

"What did you say?" His eyes darkened.

"Nothing, forget it."

"Ju. Don't ever question my commitment. This is only temporary. Once I get the new barber shop up and running things will go back to normal. I'm doing my best. What I need is for you to be patient with me."

"Whatever."

"Come on Ju."

"Look, I have to go. We can finish this conversation tonight. I'll text you when I pick up little man."

"Love you Ju."

"I love you. Be safe." His eyes remained on me until I exited the room. Brandon hated when I gave him attitude and he couldn't tame me. He would never admit it, but he also couldn't stand when I was mad at him. I was used to our routine. That had changed when he decided to open up another barbershop, but Brandon always put us first, so I was going to do my best to be patient no matter how frustrating the situation was.

When I finally arrived to work, Draya and Megan were in the conference room with one of our clients. It looked like they were going over the mockups I emailed to Draya while I was still home. The meeting seemed to be going well based on their interactions, so I quickly walked to my office to put up my bags and grabbed myself a cup of coffee before joining the meeting.

"Good morning. Thank you for being patient and getting started without me."

"No worries. Draya and Megan have been a pleasure and these mockups are exactly what I've been looking for. With a few minor changes it will be perfect."

"I'm still not using that picture of you and your cat." I pointed at my long-time client. She owned a crystal shop where she sold crystals, incense, sage, and other related items. Tammie was quirky and a little weird but had a gentle spirit. She *loved* cats.

"Aww come on. I still think it's a good idea."

"Nah. If you are good with everything, I will let these two wrap things up with you while I go work on my other project. If I finish early, then we can all take a few days off."

"Well get to work boss!" Megan piped up.

"Okay. I'll call you later. I have some goodies for you." Tammie replied

Four hours later, I was finishing up the mockup board I created to present to a client. They were rebranding and needed help with everything from their colors, logo, social media layouts, flyers, everything and I was more than happy to help. The popular non-profit had lost their employee who was in charge of communications and publicity, so they contracted me to get the job done. It was exciting because I knew it would open the door for more clients. My alarm alerted me that BJ would be out of school in thirty minutes, so I wrapped up everything and headed to scoop up my little man.

I approached the front desk and the receptionist couldn't even hide the disdain through her fake smile. She obviously hated when Brandon didn't pick up BJ. I was already on to her little crush. The first time I accompanied Brandon to pick him up she was smiling and batting her wing-like eye lashes until she saw me holding on to his finger. Truth be told, I don't know why she was so put off because she was not Brandon's type. This girl was tall and skinny, and Brandon preferred girls that were shorter and much thicker, but she was looking at me like I stole her man.

"Good afternoon."

"Yes, and you are here for?"

"Um I am here for Brandon Smith Jr.?" I rolled my eyes at her acting like she didn't know who I was by now.

"Hmph. Have a seat I will notify his teacher." I busied myself by staring at the colorful flyers pinned on the corkboard as if I hadn't seen them already. What I was really doing was avoiding eye contact with this chick because if she gave me the stank face one more time, I was going to put her in her place.

"JuJu! JuJu!" BJ was all smiles as he ran towards me full speed. The teacher's assistant struggled to keep up. He was fast for his age. I squatted down and he slammed into me, and almost took me down onto the floor.

"Hey little man! Ooof! Oh my gosh I missed you. How was school?"

"Good! Look!" He held up a drawing of a dog. BJ was obsessed with dogs lately and Brandon was considering buying him one.

"Wow! This is a work of art. We must add this to your exhibit," I spoke in a fake posh accent and he giggled. I was so smitten with this little boy. I removed his bookbag, looped it on my arm, and held my hand out for him.

"I believe that we have a date at the park Mr. Smith. Are you ready?"

"Yeah!"

"Well then, let's go have some fun."

BIZZIE

The call that I received made my stomach drop. I'd never been afraid of anything except with it came to my son. I sped through the parking lot and pulled into the first space I could find before I ran towards the emergency room entrance.

"Lord please let my son be okay." He just had to be okay. When Julissa called, she was a blubbering mess, so I had trouble putting together what happened or what condition my son was in. All I knew was that he was hurt and to get to the hospital.

"See I knew I didn't like that bitch. That's why you can't trust random hoes to look after your babies. I swear to God!"

"Yo Jay chill out. I need to fucking think." Jaynah was a mess so I decided to pick her up. I couldn't afford her wrecking out trying to get to the hospital since she wasn't the best at driving. When we reached the front desk, we were informed that they'd already taken him to the back and provided us with the room number. He was being prepped for a cast. His head rested on Julissa as he watched the doctor with tear-stained cheeks.

"Mommy! Daddy!"

"What did you do to my son, you stupid bitch? Get away from him now!" Julissa looked at Jaynah in shock, then at me. She kissed BJ on the forehead before standing up and heading towards the door."

"I- I'm sorry. It was an accident. He was..."

"Do I look like I want to hear anything you have to say? Get out

99

and stay away from my son!" Julissa took in a shaky breath and turned to me. It was evident that she was looking for me to back her up as she searched my eyes but all I could see was my son being treated for a broken arm.

"Baby I would never do anything to hurt your son. You know that. Brandon?"

I cleared my throat and shook my head. "What the hell happened? I trusted you." Her mouth fell open and tears rimmed her eyes. She quickly swiped away the first tear.

"I'm sorry. He was playing and I…"

There was a swift knock on the door before a woman walked in showing her ID badge.

"Hi, I am Lorna Murphy with DCF. Which of you are the parents of Brandon Smith Jr.?" Jaynah and I raised our hands. She turned her attention to Julissa.

"And you are?"

"Julissa. I'm his…" We locked eyes and she hesitated. "I'm his girlfriend, Julissa Rivera. I was supervising BJ when he fell."

"Tuh! Fell. That's what you say." Jaynah rolled her eyes and took Julissa's place sitting next to BJ.

"Okay Ms. Rivera. I need to speak with you first in private." Julissa nodded and followed her out of the room. She didn't look to me this time.

"She did something to my baby. I just know she did. That girl probably never wanted me to have him because she wanted you all to herself."

"Gone with that Jay. Don't talk like that in front of him."

"Why not? Hey baby you want to tell mommy what happened?"

"Um, I fell… I flew." *Fuck.* I knew where he was going with this, especially with the guilty expression on his face.

"Flew? BJ, baby, did you jump from the swing?" Jaynah spoke in a soothing tone.

He nodded his little head and avoided looking up at me.

"Hey, son. It's okay, daddy's not mad. Daddy's just glad that you're okay, but you have to stop doing that. You see what happened when you didn't listen?"

He nodded and started crying.

"Ju in trouble?" I kissed the top of his forehead and shook my head.

"No, but we all owe her an apology. I think you gave her a scare and we weren't very nice to her, your mom and I." Jaynah kissed her teeth and I looked at her. "You heard your son. I think you owe her an apology. Accidents happen."

"And what about you? I didn't see you jumping to her defense."

"I'm going to smooth things over with her."

"Alrighty, he is ready to go. I am going to have a prescription drawn up for him. I just need you all to fill out the remaining paperwork. There was some information that the other young lady didn't know."

"Thanks doc."

While Jaynah was focusing on the paperwork I got a permanent marker from the nurse's station so I could be the first person to sign my son's cast. He'd also asked me to draw a picture which I was finishing up when the social worker came back in. We stepped out reluctantly and allowed her to sit with BJ. It wasn't even five minutes when she opened the door to let us know she was finished.

"Okay. From what I've discussed with Ms. Rivera, the doctor and BJ her description of what happened seems to match his injury. She said that they were at the park and he jumped off the swing and that's not his first time." I dropped my head because she just confirmed that I'd fucked up with how I handled things.

"Nah, it ain't. We've been working on getting him to stop."

"Well I am sure this little scare will deter him." She looked at BJ and smiled.

"Where did she go?"

"She left as soon as we were done. Mentioned that it was best that she left."

"Shit." *She was going to leave me.* That was all I could think. My heart dropped and I instantly felt the need to get home as soon as possible, but it wasn't possible. BJ was my priority right now. I immediately pulled my phone out of my pocket and tried to call Julissa, but I got her voicemail. I heard Jaynah suck her teeth before she headed back into the room to get BJ ready to go.

By the time I got Jaynah home and BJ settled in bed I came home to an empty house. The shit was weird. The place was void of her energy and she hadn't returned any of my calls or texts. I sat in the living room with the TV on waiting for her to walk through the front door, but she never did.

BIZZIE

A whole ass week had gone by and I hadn't heard or seen Julissa. Since Jaynah couldn't afford to take off, BJ had been staying with me. I was able to work from home and care for him. He asked where Ju was every day she didn't come and at this point, I was running out of things to tell him. He needed to connect with her following his accident; she was there for him through it all. Hell, I needed to connect with her. My attempt at getting information from Lauryn was feeble since she was giving me the silent treatment.

After all I'd done to convince her that she was safe with me and I'd always have her back I turned around and sided with Jaynah when things got rough. I did exactly what I promised her I wouldn't do. I didn't care if she was pissed with me, I could handle her anger, sometimes. What I couldn't handle was hurting her. She was hurt and she didn't have to tell me that. It was all over her face at the hospital and I ignored it.

"Nigga are you even paying attention? B... B!" Eric scowled.

"What?"

"The apartment building. Are you in or not?" Kevin truly looked like he was concerned for me.

"Yeah. I'm in." Eric and Kevin came over to show me pictures and video footage of these old apartment buildings the city was planning on demolishing. We were willing to buy them and fix them up as to not displace the people. That was what we'd been focusing on lately. Too many developers were coming into our community building new apartments and homes that the people couldn't afford, therefore contributing to the gentrification of the hood.

"Alright then, pay attention."

"Where is she E?" Eric smirked and shook his head.

"Look I have told all of y'all to leave me out of this. It's always something."

"Something like what? Lauryn can't be involving herself in my business..."

"Nah, you wrong there. This ain't got shit to do with you. Julissa is her friend first. Her best friend since high school."

"Man, y'all get the fuck out!" I stood up from where I sat.

"You need to chill the fuck out B." Eric's jaw twitched, and he stared up at me.

"Bitch I don't work for you no more. Get the fuck out!"

"Alright B, but you're tripping. I'll have my assistant submit the paperwork to the management company. Have your ass in the meeting next week. Oh, eat a damn Snickers or something and get out your damn feelings. That and the fact that my God son is in the other room watching cartoons is the only reason we ain't fucking up this room right now."

"Man whatever. Why y'all still here?"

Eric and Kevin gathered their shit and made their way out without me seeing them to the door. Eric was right, I was in my feelings, but I felt like I had every right to be. I hadn't felt the slick warm walls or heard the voice of my woman in a week. I was backed up and cranky. The sound of the laughter reminded me that my son deserved to have me at my best. Putting a smile on my face, I stood up, stretched my limbs and joined my son in front of the TV.

After a couple of Disney movies and homemade cheese pizza BJ was sprawled out in his bed knocked out. He could barely keep his eyes open during his bath. I sat in his room just watching him as he slept. Watching him brought me peace and I needed it to sleep. When I made it to my room, I double checked my phone for any missed calls or messages from Julissa. Disappointment fell over me when I saw that I only had a text from my boy E, but when I opened it, I couldn't help the smile that formed on my weary face.

Eric: Ju is at the house.

Me: Bet. Thanks bro.

I paced my bedroom floor biting on my nail trying to figure out my next move. There was no way I could just run over there with my son sleeping in his room, but I couldn't go another night without her in this bed next to me. This woman was my world. She meant everything to me and I refused to screw it up again.

Me: Yo Jay.

Jaynah: Yes.

Me: I need you to take BJ for the night. I will pick him up from school.

Jaynah: Fine Brandon.

Me: Be there in fifteen minutes.

Lauryn was making her way to the door as soon as I entered my code and made my way in the house. She planted her short ass right in front of me in an attempt to block my path.

"She doesn't want to see you right now Biz."

"What? Come on Lauryn stop playing. This has nothing to do with you. Where's your husband?"

"He ain't here and can't help you. I know he told you where she was." Lauryn pointed at me and rolled her neck as she spoke.

I gritted my teeth. "Sis." Lauryn crossed her arms and rolled her neck again. I loved this woman, but she could frustrate Jesus.

"I could do this all-night Brandon." She sung my name and I was coming unhinged.

"SHE'S MY FUCKING WIFE LAURYN!"

Lauryn's eyes damn neared popped out of her head and she took a step back. Yeah, we were keeping it a secret and were planning to surprise everyone together when she got back on good terms with her family. She was planning this huge dinner party at our house.

"What? She would never... When?" She looked at me incredulously.

"Vegas Lauryn." Without another word she spun around on her

heels and stomped upstairs. I followed her into one of the guest suites. Julissa was sitting on the floor drawing. She jumped at the sound of Lauryn's voice.

"Seriously Ju? MARRIED? And you didn't think that your best friend should know!? I cannot..."

"Sis! Can we have some privacy. Please." I stepped around Lauryn before facing her.

"Yeah, of course. I'm sorry."

I sat on the bed and watched my wife continue to draw and not acknowledge my presence.

"Ju look at me. Please." And there they were. Those beautiful brown sugar eyes.

"I'm sorry. I should have had your back and I was wrong. Getting your call was terrifying and... No excuses. I should have had your back and I need you back home. I miss you. BJ misses you too. He asks about you every day."

"I love BJ like he's my own. Did you not once consider how I was feeling? Did you not think that I was scared? He was in so much pain and I was so freaked out that one of the moms at the park had to drive me and her husband followed with my car. I was scared and I- I blamed myself, but I never thought that you would."

"I'm sorry baby, but I came home to you, to my wife, that same night and you were gone. That shit can't happen again. We are married and we work through our shit, not leave. Neither of us are allowed to check out; we are a team. You and I are one and I ain't going anywhere. Even when your bratty ass ticks me off. I need you to believe me and trust me when I say this is it. We are officially family now." I reached into my pocket and slipped her ring on her finger. "Don't ever take this off again." Julissa smiled and jumped up into my lap. I wrapped her in a tight embrace and relished in her scent; glad to have her safely in my arms again. Her lips brushed against mine and I kissed her. She eagerly opened up and allowed my tongue to explore her sweet mouth. I abruptly pulled back and laughed when her eyes slowly fluttered open.

"Now get your shit so we can go home and have make up sex. We got a new bed to break in."

"Girl you heard him! Hurry up and go get that tune up." Julissa cut her eyes at Lauryn. I pulled Lauryn out of the room before these two ended up fighting.

"I'm sorry Brandon. There was no way I would have let her stay here this long had I known that you two were married."

"It's cool."

"If it means anything to you, I think you're good for her. You two are good for each other. Take care of my friend."

"Don't worry your pretty little head nosey. Ya bestie is in good hands."

JULISSA

Love looked good on us. That's what Lauryn had declared the last time we all hung out together and I couldn't deny it. I'd stopped looking for reasons why our relationship wouldn't survive and started counting all the ways that we could overcome any obstacle. We were both happy, in love, and had successful businesses. Brandon and I were still newlyweds trying to figure things out, like me legally changing my last name, but we'd formed a routine that worked for us. Even Jaynah had stopped worrying about us and found her some new business aka penis. I ain't mad at her though because the man was fine. Life had been good, and I was grateful for all my blessings. Every day I discovered something new about my husband, so it never got boring. Surprisingly, Brandon had dragged me out of bed at the crack of dawn for breakfast. This gesture made me suspicious because he was a grouch in the morning. He took me to eat at my favorite breakfast/brunch spot. On the way back home, I let myself get caught up in good music and a full belly. When he past our exit I sat up.

"Where are we going?"

"To see your peeps."

"Lauryn and Eric?"

"Your family."

"What? Brandon, no. Stop playing and turn around." I sat up in my seat. The thought of seeing my family already had me on edge.

"Nah. It's already fucked up that I married a man's daughter without approaching him or even knowing him. We've been married going on four months now and they still don't know. Christmas is right around the corner."

"Actually, nobody knew."

Brandon glared at me. "Alright. Keep that up with your smart ass and I got something for you later."

"You promise?" I flirted with my husband. I loved saying that. I was Mrs. Brandon Smith and it was the best feeling in the world, except when he was trying to boss up on me.

"Look Ju. I need for you to do this. I know that I act like I don't care but I want to get to know your family and welcome them as a part of mine. The idea of having a family... I don't know, the thought of it feels good and I want to have kids with you. They should be born into a situation where they have grandparents, aunties, and uncles who their mom is on good terms with."

Brandon baring his soul always did something to me. He was so used to holding everything in, but he now trusted me with his darkest secrets and memories. I made him comfortable enough to share how he felt.

"Fine." I huffed. Knowing that I was minutes away from my childhood home made my stomach do somersaults. I was nervous. Not only was I popping up after months of no communication, but I was coming with a husband they knew nothing about. My younger sister had met Brandon at Lauryn's wedding, but last she knew we'd broken up. Brandon wanted family and I was hoping that mine didn't make him feel unwanted.

We pulled up to my family's modest five-bedroom home. It was on a huge piece of land. My parents were known for spending more money on their children than on themselves.

"This is nice. Not what I was expecting, but it's nice."

"What were you expecting? Some monstrosity of a house with fountains and an electric gate."

"Yeah or something close to that based on your bougie ass condo. I mean it's huge but humble."

"Whatever." Brandon looked over at me and kissed my hand.

"You ready?"

"If I say no can we go back home?"

"Nope. Come on scary cat." He turned off the car and got out. I stayed seated until he came around and opened the door for me.

"You smell good baby." He flashed me the sexiest smile in return. That got a smile out of me.

"Boy let's go."

I used my key to let us in. Loud voices were coming from the family room.

"Mamí!" I yelled as I led us to where everyone was gathered. Everyone was over, including my sister's husbands and kids.

"Tía!" They yelled in unison before attacking me. I hugged and kissed each and every one of them.

"Hey babies. Tía JuJu missed y'all so much!" While the kids teemed with excitement the adults were silent. All conversation had stopped. I stood up and faced my family.

"Tía, who is he?"

"Um well, that's part of the reason why I'm here. Hi papí, mamí, everyone."

"Hey JuJu." Theresa, my youngest sister, rushed across the room and embraced me. It felt good to have my sister in my arms. It wasn't until then that I realized how much I missed my family. She looked up at Brandon and smirked.

"I remember you. Hey."

"Hi Theresa. It's good to see you again."

"Well it seems like you are acquainted with two of my daughters, but I still have no idea who you are young man." My father stood up and approached us. I stepped forward to speak but Brandon clutched my hand and tugged me back. He extended his hand to my father who only stared at it.

"Good afternoon Mr. Rivera, Mrs. Rivera. I'm Brandon Smith. Julissa's husband."

"What!? The women screamed but stilled when my dad glared at them; it was a silent warning.

"What did you say to me young man?"

"Papí we're married. Um, I got married a few months ago."

"MONTHS! You go months without speaking to any of us and

then you return and announce that you are married to some strange man? What did I do to deserve such an ungrateful and disappointing daughter? You should have just stayed away."

"Juan! Enough." My mother gasped and jumped up from her seat.

"Dad... I." The words would not come. My father's words had cut me deep.

"With all due respect sir, I'm not going to stand here and let you disrespect my wife. I will defend her against anyone who tries to make her feel that she is anything less than the charismatic, intelligent, beautiful, independent woman that she is. We ain't come here for that. I didn't bring her here to fight or to be talked to like she ain't shit."

"Baby..." I rubbed his back to calm the beast. He took a few deep breaths.

"I'm sorry. Please excuse my language. All I am saying is that she misses and needs her family, so here we are." The room was so quiet you could hear a pin drop. My brothers-in-law ushered the kids upstairs. My father scoffed and finally shook Brandon's hand when he held it out again.

"You got balls; I like that. Come, let's talk out back." Brandon kissed me on the top of my head then followed my dad outside. My mother and sisters swarmed me once it was just us women.

"Omg Ju! He is so big!"

"And the way he looks at you!"

"And the way he stood up to papí. Christian would never!" They were all speaking at the same time and I struggled to keep up. They were literally swooning over my husband. My mom held her hand up to settle the room.

"Are you happy míja?"

I nodded. "Yes I am. I've never been with a man that I could count on or fully be myself with, with no apologies. Well actually there was one potential..."

"What happened to him?"

"Brandon did." We all giggled and got comfortable so we could play catch up. It felt good to have this quality time with my mother and sisters. We hadn't been together like this in a very long time.

"Julissa, we, I owe you an apology. We were wrong. You and your sisters were taught to be intelligent independent women, but you were always so head-strong and independent. Your father and I pushing the topic of marriage sent mixed signals. Although I didn't agree with the path you decided to take, I should have supported you as your mother. That won't happen again. No matter what was said in the heat of the moment we've always been proud of you. Your father and I should have never judged you or pushed you to get married, but I am glad that you found someone. I can tell that you are safe with him and we won't have to worry so much about you."

I stood up and allowed my mother to hug me tightly. We stayed like that for a while before we both stood back.

"Thank you, mom. I appreciate you saying that. Just trust that there is always both a method and reason to my madness."

"Aye dios mios. Let me pray for that husband of yours." My mother drew a cross over her chest and kissed it up to God while my sisters and I looked on laughing. Our head turned at the sound of the back door opening. Brandon and my father entered the family room; my dad walking straight toward me with his arms wide open. I practically fell into his embrace.

"Julissa, I am sorry for the hurtful things that I've said. Your husband sang your praises. You've accomplished a lot. He's a proud husband and I am proud of you míja."

And that was when the flood gates open and I allowed the tears to fall. I sobbed in his arms. His words where simple but held so much weight. All I ever wanted was to make my parents proud and for them to look past the negative and see all the good that I was doing.

"I love you papí."

"I love you more."

When I stepped out of my father's embrace my mom already had her arm's looped through Brandon's and was leading him to the kitchen.

"Mamí we just ate!"

"Hush niña. He's a grown man. He can always eat."

There was no lie to that, so I just shook my head and followed as we all gathered in the kitchen to have my first family dinner with my incredible, loving husband.

We stayed at my parents' house for the entire day and even then, no one wanted to leave. It hadn't felt like that in a very long time. The only thing missing was BJ. My family was so excited to meet him. Mom was already planning a family dinner.

I laid in the bed with Brandon watching a movie while he lazily ran his fingers up and down my arm. I damn near jumped out of the bed when the demon child crawled from under the bed at an inhuman like speed. Her body contorted and spasmed. Brandon damn neared cackled, releasing a loud, obnoxious laugh. I wanted to strangle him.

"It's not funny Brandon! Please find something else to watch. I slapped him on his arm. He held his stomach and struggled to catch his breath. I was starting to think he chose this movie to get a reaction out of me. I tilted my head to the side and waited for him to finish.

"Yo my bad baby. Here, you can pick the movie."

"No, I don't mind you choosing the movie as long as it is not a horror or thriller." After scrolling through the categories, we settle on a classic action flick. I snuggled back up under him.

"Thank you."

"For?"

"For today Brandon. Thank you for doing that for me. If I am honest with myself, I probably would have held off until the next year."

"You think I don't know that? That's exactly why I did what I did. I know your family may have hurt you but it's better than not having any family or a dysfunctional family. They're good people who made mistakes and I promise to protect you. I got your back."

I sat up on the bed and took the remote from him before placing it on the nightstand. A devious grin formed on my face and

I climbed on top of Brandon who looked both curious and entertained.

"I don't want to watch the movie anymore. I want to make one."

"Oh yeah?" He piped up. Those beautiful dimples revealed themselves. I felt like the luckiest woman in the world under is gaze.

"Mmmhmm." I nodded my head.

"Okay I'm with that, but I have one special request."

His hands ran up my thighs to my waist before he pulled my night gown over my head and massaged my breasts with both hands. There was a glint of mischief in my eyes just as there was in his. Brandon pulled his bottom lip into his mouth and tugged at my nipple. I moaned.

"What's that?" He sat up and nuzzled the side of my neck before he flipped me on my back.

"Let's go half on a baby."

"Brandon!"

The End

ACKNOWLEDGEMENT

I am forever humbled and forever grateful. To the friends who listened as I worked through my storylines and gave input to put my brain back on track. To those who instilled confidence with their feedback and excitement. To my fellow female authors who inspired and made this dream believable just by following theirs. To those who supported in any way.

Thank you

Be love, be light, and be safe!

CONNECT WITH TAKISHA TRENEAN

Facebook: @takishatrenean

Instagram: @takisha_trenean

Amazon: amazon.com/author/takishatrenean

www.ingramcontent.com/pod-product-compliance
Lightning Source LLC
Chambersburg PA
CBHW060234180626
46813CB00007B/3072